D1375469

MICHAEL MOORCOCK

One of England's most versatile
writers:
"Has achieved something of a *tour de force*
with his wild fantasies — he has an undeniable
ability to dream rich and wonderful dreams."
Tribune

"Mr Moorcock's romances are vividly
coloured, sensuously evocative ... impressively
single-minded and written with utter
conviction."
Fantasy and Science Fiction

"The most important successor to Mervyn
Peake and Wyndham Lewis ... The vast,
tragic and sometimes terrifying symbolism by
which Mr Moorcock continually illuminates
the metaphysical quest of his hero are a
measure of the author's remarkable talents."
J. G. Ballard

By the same author
in Mayflower Books

THE BLACK CORRIDOR
THE JEWEL IN THE SKULL
THE MAD GOD'S AMULET
THE RUNESTAFF
THE STEALER OF SOULS
STORMBRINGER
THE SWORD OF THE DAWN
THE SINGING CITADEL
THE ETERNAL CHAMPION
PHOENIX IN OBSIDIAN
BEHOLD THE MAN
THE FINAL PROGRAMME
THE TIME DWELLER
THE KNIGHT OF THE SWORDS
THE QUEEN OF THE SWORDS

The King
of the Swords

Michael Moorcock

Volume the Third of
The Books of Corum

Mayflower

Granada Publishing Limited
First published in 1972 by Mayflower Book Ltd.
3 Upper James Street, London W1R 4BP

Reprinted 1972

Copyright © Michael Moorcock 1972
Made and printed in Denmark at
A/S Uniprint, Copenhagen.
Set in Plantin

This Book is for Renata

Contents

INTRODUCTION 7

BOOK ONE

The First Chapter
The Shape on the Hill 15

The Second Chapter
The Sickness Spreads 22

The Third Chapter
Chaos Returned 28

The Fourth Chapter
A New Ally for Earl Glandyth 33

The Fifth Chapter
The Deserted City 39

The Sixth Chapter
The Weary God 45

BOOK TWO

The First Chapter
Chaos Unbounded 51

The Second Chapter
The Castle Built of Blood 56

The Third Chapter
The Rider on the Yellow Horse 61

The Fourth Chapter
The Manor in the Forest 71

The Fifth Chapter
The Lady Jane Pentallyon 76

The Sixth Chapter
Sailing on the Seas of Time 83

The Seventh Chapter
The Land of Tall Stones 88

The Eighth Chapter
Into the Small Storm 93

BOOK THREE

The First Chapter
Voilodion Ghagnasdiak 107

The Second Chapter
To Tanelorn 117

The Third Chapter
The Conjunction of the Million Spheres 121

The Fourth Chapter
The King of the Swords 128

The Fifth Chapter
The Last of Glandyth 132

EPILOGUE 141

INTRODUCTION

*In those days there were oceans of light and cities in the skies
and wild flying beasts of bronze. There were herds of crimson
cattle that roared and were taller than castles. There were
shrill, viridian things that haunted bleak rivers. It was a time
of gods, manifesting themselves upon our world in all her
aspects; a time of giants who walked on water; of mindless
sprites and misshapen creatures who could be summoned by
an ill-considered thought but driven away only on pain of
some fearful sacrifice; of magics, phantasms, unstable nature,
impossible events, insane paradoxes, dreams come true,
dreams gone awry, of nightmares assuming reality.*

*It was a rich time and a dark time. The time of the Sword
Rulers. The time when the Vadhagh and the Nhadragh,
age-old enemies, were dying. The time when Man, the slave of
fear, was emerging, unaware that much of the terror he experienced was the result of nothing else but the fact that he,
himself, had come into existence. It was one of many ironies
connected with Man (who, in those days, called his race
"Mabden").*

*The Mabden lived brief lives and bred prodigiously.
Within a few centuries they rose to dominate the westerly
continent on which they had evolved. Superstition stopped
them from sending many of their ships towards Vadhagh and
Nhadragh lands for another century or two, but gradually
they gained courage when no resistance was offered. They
began to feel jealous of the older races; they began to feel malicious.*

*The Vadhagh and the Nhadragh were not aware of this.
They had dwelt a million or more years upon the planet
which now, at last, seemed at rest. They knew of the Mabden
but considered them not greatly different from other beasts.
Though continuing to indulge their traditional hatreds of one
another, the Vadhagh and the Nhadragh spent their long
hours in considering abstractions, in the creation of works of
art and the like. Rational, sophisticated, at one with them-*

7

selves, these older races were unable to believe in the changes that had come. Thus, as it almost always is, they ignored the signs.

There was no exchange of knowledge between the two ancient enemies, even though they had fought their last battle many centuries before.

The Vadhagh lived in family groups occupying isolated castles scattered across a continent called by them Bro-an-Vadhagh. There was scarcely any communication between these families, for the Vadhagh had long since lost the impulse to travel. The Nhadragh lived in their cities built on the island in the seas to the north west of Bro-an-Vadhagh. They, also, had little contact, even with their closest kin. Both races reckoned themselves invulnerable. Both were wrong.

Upstart Man was beginning to breed and spread like a pestilence across the world. This pestilence struck down the old races wherever it touched them. And it was not only death that Man brought, but terror, too. Wilfully, he made of the older world nothing but ruins and bones. Unwittingly, he brought psychic and supernatural disruption of a magnitude which even the Great Old Gods failed to comprehend.

And the Great Old Gods began to know Fear.

And Man, slave of fear, arrogant in his ignorance, continued his stumbling progress. He was blind to the huge disruptions aroused by his apparently petty ambitions. As well, Man was deficient in sensitivity, had no awareness of the multitude of dimensions that filled the universe, each plane intersecting with several others. Not so the Vadhagh or the Nhadragh, who had known what it was to move at will between the dimensions they termed the Five Planes. They had glimpsed and understood the nature of the many planes, other than the five, through which the Earth moved.

Therefore it seemed a dreadful injustice that these wise races should perish at the hands of creatures who were still little more than animals. It was as if vultures feasted on and squabbled over the paralysed body of the youthful poet who could only stare at them with puzzled eyes as they slowly robbed him of an exquisite existence they would never appreciate, never know they were taking.

"If they valued what they stole, if they knew what they were destroying," says the old Vadhagh in the story, The Only Autumn Flower, "then I would be consoled."

It was unjust.

By creating Man, the universe had betrayed the old races.

But it was a perpetual and familiar injustice. The sentient may perceive and love the universe, but the universe cannot perceive and love the sentient. The universe sees no distinction between the multitude of creatures and elements which comprise it. All are equal. None is favoured. The universe, equipped with nothing but the materials and the power of creation, continues to create; something of this, something of that. It cannot control what it creates and it cannot, it seems, be controlled by its creations (though a few might deceive themselves otherwise). Those who curse the workings of the universe curse that which is deaf. Those who strike out at those workings fight that which is inviolate. Those who shake their fists, shake their fists at blind stars.

But this does not mean that there are some who will not try to do battle with and destroy the invulnerable.

There will always be such beings, sometimes beings of great wisdom, who cannot bear to believe in an insouciant universe.

Prince Corum Jhaelen Irsei was one of these. Perhaps the last of the Vadhagh Race, he was sometimes known as the Prince in the Scarlet Robe.

This chronicle concerns him.

We have already learned how the Mabden followers of Earl Glandyth-a-Krae (who called themselves the Denle-dhyssi — or Murderers) killed Prince Corum's relatives and his nearest kin and thus taught the Prince in the Scarlet Robe how to hate, how to kill and how to desire vengeance. We have heard how Glandyth tortured Corum and took away a hand and an eye and how Corum was rescued by the Giant of Laahr and taken to the castle of the Margravine Rhalina — a castle set upon a mount surrounded by the sea. Though Rhalina was a Mabden woman (of the gentler folk of Lywm-an-Esh) Corum and she fell in love. When Glandyth roused the Pony Tribes, the forest barbarians, to attack the Margravine's castle, she and Corum sought supernatural aid and thus fell into the hands of the sorcerer Shool, whose domain was the island called Svi-an-Fanla-Brool — Home of the Gorged God. And now Corum had direct experience of the morbid, unfamiliar powers at work in the world. Shool spoke of dreams and realities. ("I see you are beginning to argue in Mabden terms," he told Corum. "It is just as well for you, if

9

you wish to survive in this Mabden dream." — *"It is a dream ...?"* said Corum — *"Of sorts. Real enough. It is what you might call the dream of a God. There again you might say that it is a dream that a God has allowed to become reality. I refer of course to the Knight of the Swords who rules the Five Planes.")*

With Rhalina his prisoner Shool could make a bargain with Corum. He gave him two gifts — the Hand of Kwll and the Eye of Thynn — to replace his own missing organs. These jewelled and alien things were once the property of two brother gods known as the Lost Gods since they mysteriously vanished.

Now Shool told Corum what he must do if he wished to see Rhalina saved. Corum must go to the Realm of the Knight of the Swords — Lord Arioch of Chaos who ruled the Five Planes since he had wrested them from the control of Lord Arkyn of Law. There Corum must find the heart of the Knight of the Swords — a thing which was kept in a tower of his castle and which enabled him to take material shape on Earth and thus wield power (without a material shape — or a number of them — the Lords of Chaos could not rule mortals).

With little hope Corum set off in a boat for the domain of Arioch but on his way was wrecked when a huge giant passed by him, merely fishing. In the land of the strange Raghadda-Kheta he discovered that the Eye could summon dreadful beings from those worlds to aid him — also the hand seemed to sense danger before it came and was ruthless in slaying even when Corum did not desire to slay. Then he realised that, by accepting Shool's gifts, he had accepted the logic of Shool's world and could not escape from it now.

During these adventures Corum learned of the eternal struggle between Law and Chaos. A cheerful traveller from Lywm-an-Esh enlightened him. It was, he said, "the Chaos Lords' will that rules you. Arioch is one of them. Long since there was a war between the forces of Order and the forces of Chaos. The forces of Chaos won and came to dominate the Fifteen Planes and, as I understand it, much that lies beyond them. Some say that Order was defeated completely and all her Gods vanished. They say the Cosmic Balance tipped too far in one direction and that is why there are so many arbitrary events taking place in the world. They say that once the world was round instead of dish-shaped ..." — "Some Vadhagh legends say it was once round," Corum informed him. — "Aye. Well, the Vadhagh began their rise before Order was banished. That it why the Sword Rulers hate the old races so much. They are not their creation at all. But the Great Gods are not allowed to interfere too directly in mortal affairs, so they have worked through the Mabden, chiefly ..." — Corum said: "is this the truth?" — Hanafax shrugged. "It is a truth."

Later, in the Flamelands where the blind queen Ooresé lived, Corum saw a mysterious figure who almost immediately vanished after he had slain poor Hanafax with the Hand of Kwll (which knew Hanafax would betray him). He learned that Arioch was the Knight of the Swords and that Xiombarg was the Queen of the Swords ruling the next group of Five Planes, while the most powerful Sword Ruler of all ruled the last of the Five Planes — Mabelode, King of the Swords. Corum learned that all the hearts of the Sword Rulers were hidden where even they could not touch them. But after further adventures in Arioch's castle, he at last succeeded in finding the heart of the Knight of the Swords and, to save his life, destroyed it, thus banishing Arioch to limbo and allowing Arkyn of Law to return to occupy his old castle. But Corum had earned the Bane of the Sword Rulers and by destroying Arioch's heart had set a pattern of destiny for himself. A voice told him: "Neither Law nor Chaos must dominate the destinies of the mortal planes. There must be equilibrium." But it seemed to Corum that there was no equilibrium, that Chaos ruled All. "The balance sometimes tips," replied the voice. "It must be righted. And that is the power of mortals, to adjust the balance. You have begun the work already. Now you must continue until it is finished. You may perish before it is complete, but some other will follow you."

Corum shouted: "I do not want this. I cannot bear such a burden."

The voice replied:

— "YOU MUST!"

And then Corum returned to find Shool's power gone and Thalina free.

They returned to the lovely castle on Moidel's Mount, knowing that they were no longer in any sense in control of their own fates.

Soon the Wading God was seen again, fishing the seas near Moidel's Mount, forever discarding his catch and casting for a new one. An omen, they knew. And that night there was a

11

knocking on the door of Moidel's Castle and a young stranger presented himself to them — a dandy who had as a pet a little winged cat. This was Jhary-a-Conel who announced his profession as a "Companion to Champions" and seemed to know a great deal of Corum's destiny, not to mention his own. With the help of the little cat they learned of the great Mabden massing at Kalenwyr, of the intention of the Mabden to march against Lywm-an-Esh and destroy that land because it had adopted Vadhagh ways. The people of the castle knew that they would be swept away by such a mighty advance and they abandoned Moidel's Mount, going by ship to Lywm-an-Esh to discover that the invasion was already taking place on some coasts and that the followers of Law and Chaos were divided, fighting. In the capital, Halwyg-nan-Vake, they saw the king and learned that Arkyn would speak with them at his Temple. Here Arkyn told them to enter Xiombarg's plane and seek out the City in the Pyramid, that this city would aid them. On Xiombarg's plane they encountered many strange marvels, horrible examples of the power of Chaos — the Lake of Voices, the White River and many other things — until they found the City in The Pyramid. This strange city of metal was peopled by Vadhagh and Corum learned that they had left their own plane centuries before but had been unable to return. Xiombarg began to attack the City and Corum and his companions fled through the planes to Halwyg to find it under dire siege. At last the means to bring the City in the Pyramid back to its own plane was found and they broke through, bringing destruction to the Mabden and forever wiping out the threat. Angered, Xiombarg followed — breaking the paramount rule of the Cosmic Balance — and was thus destroyed. It seemed that a wonderful new era of peace had been granted to them all. But Earl Glandyth-a-Krae, who hated Corum most fiercely, had escaped the destruction of his folk. And he planned revenge.

— The Book of Corum

BOOK ONE

*In which Prince Corum sees serenity
transformed into strife*

The First Chapter

THE SHAPE ON THE HILL

Not long since men had died here and others had expected to die. But now King Onald's palace was repaired, repainted, covered once more in flowers, and the battlements had once again become balconies and bowers. But King Onald of Lywm-an-Esh would not see his ruined Halwyg-nan-Vake reborn, for he, too, had been slain in the siege and his mother ruled as regent till his son should come of age. Scaffolding lingered in some parts of the Floral City, for King Lyr-a-Brode and his barbarians had done much damage. New sculptures were being erected, fresh fountains made, and it was now plain that Halwyg's quiet magnificence would be yet finer than before. So it was across all the land of Lywm-an-Esh.

And so it was beyond the sea, in Bro-an-Vadhagh. The Mabden had been driven back to the land from which they had first come, Bro-an-Mabden, grim continent to the North East. And their fear of the power of the Vadhagh was strong again.

In the sweet land of gentle hills and deep, comforting forests and placid rivers and soft valleys which was Bro-an-Vadhagh only the ruins of gloomy Kalenwyr remained — ruins avoided but remembered.

And off the coast, on the Nhadragh Isles, the few who had survived the Mabden killings — frightened, degenerate creatures — were allowed to live out their lives. Perhaps these wretched Nhadragh would breed prouder children and their race would flourish again, as it had in its centuries of glory, before too many years passed.

The world returned to peace. The people who had come back to this place in the magical Gwlãs-cor-Gwrys, the City in the Pyramid, set to work to restore the ravaged Vadhagh castles and lands. They abandoned their strange city of metal in favour of the traditional homes of their Vadhagh ancestors. Presently Gwlãs-cor-Gwrys was all but deserted, standing amongst the pines of a remote forest, not far from one of the broken Mabden fortresses.

15

It seemed that a wonderful new age of peace had dawned both for the Mabden of Lywm-an-Esh and for the Vadhagh who had been that land's saviours. The threat of Chaos was forgotten. Now two out of three Realms — ten out of fifteen planes — were ruled by Law. Surely, therefore, Law was stronger?

Syrely, thought so. Queen Crief, the Regent of Lywm-an-Esh thought so and told her grandson, King Analt that it was so and the little king told his subjects that it was so. Prince Surette Hasdun Nury, ex-commander of gwlås-cor-Gwrys, believed it pretty much. The rest of the Vadhagh believed it, too.

There was one Vadhagh, however, who was not sure. He was unlike others of his race, though he had the same tall beauty of form, the tapering head, the gold-flecked rose-pink skin, fair hair and almond-shaped yellow and purple eyes. But instead of a right eye he had an object like the jewelled eye of a fly and instead of a left hand he had what appeared to be a six-fingered guantlet of similar design, encrusted with dark jewels. Upon his back he wore a scarlet robe and he was Corum Jhaelen Irsei, who had slain gods and been instrumental in banishing others, who desired nothing but peace but could not trust the peace he had, who hated his alien eye and his alien hand, though they had saved his life many times and thus had saved both Lywm-an-Esh and Bro-an-Vadhagh and furthered the Cause of Law.

Yet even Corum, burdened by his destiny, knew joy as he saw his old home reborn, for they were building Castle Erorn again on the headland where she had stood for centuries before Glandyth-a-Krae had razed her. Corum remembered every detail of his ancient family home and his pleasure grew as the castle grew. Slender, tinted towers stood again against the sky and overlooked the sea which was all boisterous white and green and leapt about the rocks below and in and out of the great sea-caves as if it danced with delight at Erorn's return to the eminence.

And inside the ingenuity and skills of the craftsmen of Gwlås-cor-Gwrys had wrought the sensitive walls which would change shape and colour with every change in the elements, the musical instruments of crystal and water which would play tunes according to the manner in which they were arranged. But they could not replace the paintings and the sculpture and the manuscripts which Corum and Corum's

16

ancestors had created in more innocent times, for Glandyth-a-Krae had destroyed them when he had destroyed Corum's father, Prince Khlonskey, and his mother, Colatalarna, his twin sisters, his uncle, his cousin and their retainers.

When he thought of all that was lost Corum felt a return of his old hatred of the Mabden Earl. Glandyth's body had not been found amongst those who had died at Halwyg, neither had they found the bodies of his charioteers, his Denledhyssi. Glandyth had vanished — or perhaps he and his men had died in some remote battle. It required all Corum's self-discipline not to let his mind dwell on Glandyth and what Glandyth had done. He preferred to think of ways of making Castle Erorn still more beautiful so that his wife and his love Rhalina, Margravine of Allomglyl, would be even more enraptured and would forget that when they had found her castle it had been torn down by Glandyth so thoroughly that only a few stones of it could be seen in the shallows at the bottom of Moidel's Mount.

Jhary-a-Conel, who rarely admitted such a thing, was impressed by Castle Erorn. It inspired him, he said, and he took to writing sonnets which, somewhat insistently, he would often read to them. And he painted passable portraits of Corum in his scarlet robe and of Rhalina in her gown of blue brocade and he painted a fair quantity of self-portraits which they would come across in more than one chamber of Castle Erorn. And Jhary would also pass his time designing splendid clothes for himself, sometimes making whole wardrobes, even trying new hats (though he was much attached to his old one and always returned to it). His little black and white cat with the black and white wings would fly through the rooms sometimes, but most often it would be discovered sleeping somewhere where it was most inconvenient for it to sleep.

And so they passed their days.

The coastline on which Castle Erorn was built was well-known for the softness of its summers and the mildness of its winters. Two, sometimes three, crops could be grown the year round in normal times and there was usually little frost and one snowfall in the coldest month. Often it did not snow at all. But the winter after Erorn was completed the snow began to fall early and did not stop until the oaks and the pines and the birches bent beneath huge burdens of glittering whiteness or were hidden altogether. The snow was so deep that a mounted man could not see above it in some places, and although the sun shone clear and red through the day it dit not melt the snow much and that which did melt was soon replaced by another fall.

To Corum there was a hint of something ominous in this unexpected weather. They were snug enough in their castle and had no lack of provisions and sometimes a Sky Ship would bring a visitor from one of the other newly rebuilt castles. The recently settled Vadhagh had not given up their ships of the air when they had left Gwlãs-cor-Gwrys. Thus there was no danger of losing contact with the outside world. But still Corum fretted and Jhary watched him with a certain amusement, while Rhalina took his state of mind more seriously and was careful to soothe him whenever possible, for she thought he brooded on Glandyth again.

One day Corum and Jhary stood on the balcony of a tall tower and looked inland at the wide expanse of whiteness.

"Why should I be troubled by the weather?" Corum asked Jhary. "I suspect the hand of gods in everything, these days. Why should gods bother to make it snow?"

Jhary shrugged. "You'll remember that under Law the world was said to be round. Perhaps it is round now, again, and the result of this roundness is a change in the weather you may expect in these parts."

Corum shook his head in puzzlement, hardly hearing Jhary's words. He leaned on a snowy parapet, blinking in the snow's glare. Far away there was a line of hills, as white as everything else in that landscape. He looked toward the hills. "When Bwydyth-a-Horn came visiting last week he said that it was the same over the whole land of Bro-an-Vadhagh. One cannot help but seek significance in so strange an event." He sniffed the cold, clean air. "Yet why should Chaos send a little snow, since it inconveniences no one."

"It might inconvenience the farmers of Lywm-an-Esh," Jhary said.

"True — but Lywm-an-Esh has not had this especially heavy snowfall. It was as if something sought to — to freeze us — to paralyse us ..."

"Chaos would choose more spectacular displays than a heavy fall of snow," Jhary pointed out.

"Unless it was the best they could do, now that Law rules two of the Realms."

"I am unconvinced. I think that, if anything, this is Law's doing. The result of a few minor geographical changes involved in ridding our Five Planes of the last effects of Chaos."

"I agree that that is the most logical explanation," Corum nodded.

"If an explanation is needed at all."

"Aye. I'm over-suspicious. You are probably right." He began to turn back to the entrance of the tower but then felt Jhary's hand on his arm. "What is it?"

Jhary's voice was quiet. "Look at the hills."

"The hills?" Corum peered into the distance. And a shock went through him. Something moved there. At first he thought it must be some forest animal — a fox, perhaps, hunting for food. But it was too large. It was too large to be a man — even a large man mounted on a horse. The shape was familiar, yet he could not remember where he had seen it before. It flickered, as if only partly in this plane and partly in another. It began to move away from them, towards the north. It paused and perhaps it turned, for Corum felt that something peered at him. Involuntarily his jewelled hand went to his jewelled eye, fingering the jewelled patch which covered it and stopped him from seeing into that terrible netherworld from which he had, in the past, summoned supernatural allies. With an effort he lowered his hand. Did he associate that shape with something he had seen in the netherworld? Or perhaps it was some creature of Chaos, returned to make war on Erorn?

"I cannot make anything of it," Jhary said. "Is it a beast or a man?"

Corum found difficulty in replying. "Neither, I think," he said at last.

The shape resumed its original direction, crossing over the brow of the hill and vanishing.

"We still have that Sky Ship below," Jhary said. "Shall we follow the thing?"

Corum's throat was dry. "No," he said.

"Did you know what it was, Corum? Did you recognise it?"

"I have seen it before. But I do not remember where or in what circumstances. Did it — did it look at me, Jhary, or did I imagine that."

19

"I understand you. A peculiar sensation — the sort of sensation one has when one meets another's eyes by accident."

"Aye — something of the sort."

"I wonder what it could want with us or if it is connected with this snowfall in any way."

"I do not associate it with snow. I think rather of — fire! I remember! I remember where I saw it — or something like it — in the Flamelands, after I had strangled — after this hand of mine had strangled — Hanafax. I told you of that!"

Shuddering, he remembered the scene. The Hand of Kwll squeezing the life from the struggling, shrieking Hanafax, who had done Corum no harm at all. The roaring flames. The corpse. The blind Queen Ooresé with her impassive face. The hill. The smoke. A figure standing on the hill watching him. A figure obscured by a sudden drift of smoke.

"Perhaps it is only madness," he murmured. "My conscience reminding me of the innocent soul I took when I slew Hanafax. Perhaps I am remembering my guilt and see that guilt as an accusing figure on a hillside."

"A pretty theory," said Jhary almost grimly. "But I had nothing to do with the slaying of Hanafax and neither do I suffer from this guilt you people always speak of. I saw the figure first, Corum."

"So you did. So you did." His head bowed, Corum stumbled through the door of the tower. From his mortal eye streamed tears.

As Jhary closed the door behind them, Corum turned on the stairs and stared up at his friend.

"Then what was it, Jhary?"

"I know not, Corum."

"But you know so much."

"And I forget much. I am not a hero. I am a companion to heroes. I admire. I marvel. I offer sage advice which is rarely taken. I sympathise. I save lives. I express the fears heroes cannot express. I counscil caution ..."

"Enough, Jhary. Do you jest?"

"I suppose I jest. I, too, am tired, my friend.

I am tired of the company of gloomy heroes, of those who are doomed to terrible destinies — not to mention a lack of humour. I would have the company of ordinary men for a while. I would drink in taverns. Tell obscene stories. Fart. Lose my head to a doxie ..."

"Jhary! You do not jest! Why are you saying these things?"

"Because I am weary of …" Jhary frowned. "Why, indeed, Prince Corum? It is not like me, at all. That carping voice — was mine!"

"Aye. It was." Corum's frown matched Jhary's. "And I liked it not at all. Why, if you sought to provoke me, Jhary, then …"

"Wait!" Jhary raised his hand to his head. "Wait, Corum. I feel as if something seeks possession of my mind, seeks to turn me against my friends. Concentrate. Do you not feel the same thing?"

Corum glared at Jhary for a moment and then his face lost its anger and became puzzled. "Aye. You are right. A kind of nagging shadow at the back of my head. It hints at hatred, contention. Is it the influence of the thing we saw on the hill?"

Jhary shook his head. "Who knows? I apologise for my outburst. I do not believe that it was myself speaking to you."

"I, too, apologise. Let us hope the shadow disappears."

In thoughtful silence they descended to the main part of the castle. The walls were silvery, shimmering. It meant that the snow had begun to fall outside once more.

Rhalina met them in one of the galleries where fountains and crystals sang softly a work by Corum's father, a love song to Corum's mother. It was soothing and Corum managed to smile at her.

"Corum," she said. "A few moments ago I was seized with a strange fury. I cannot explain it. I was tempted to hit one of the retainers. I …"

He took her in his arms. He kissed her brow. "I know. Jhary and I experienced the same thing. I fear that Chaos works subtly in us, turning us against each other. We must resist such impulses. We must try to find their cause. Something wishes us to destroy one another, I think."

There was horror in her eyes. "Oh, Corum …"

"We must resist," he said again.

Jhary scratched his nose, himself once more. He raised an eyebrow. "I wonder if we are the only folk who suffer this — this possession. What if it has seized the whole land, Corum?"

The Second Chapter

THE SICKNESS SPREADS

It was in the night that the worst thoughts came to Corum as he lay in bed beside Rhalina. Sometimes his visions were of his hated enemy Glandyth-a-Krae, but sometimes they were of Lord Arkyn of Law whom he was now beginning to blame for all his hardships and miseries, and sometimes they were of Jhary-a-Conel whose easy irony was now seen as facetious malice, and sometimes they were of Rhalina whom he decided had snared him, directed him away from his true destiny. And these latter visions were the worst and he fought against them more fiercely even than the other. He would feel his face twist with hatred, his fingers clench, his lips snarl, his body shake with rage and a wish to destroy. All through the nights he would fight these terrible impulses and he knew that as he fought so did Rhalina — fighting the fury welling up inside her own head. Irrational fury — rage which had no purpose and yet which would focus on anything and seek to vent itself.

Bloody visions. Visions of torturing and maiming worse than Glandyth had ever performed on him. And *he* was the torturer and those he tortured were those he loved most.

Many a night he would awake skrieking. Crying aloud the single word: "No! No! No!" he would leap from his bed and glare down at Rhalina.

And Rhalina would glare back.

Rhalina's lips would curl back from her white teeth. Rhalina's nostrils would flare like those of a beast. And strange sounds would come from her throat.

Then he would fight off the impulses and cry to her, remind her of what was happening to them. And they would lie in each other's arms, drained of emotion.

The snow had begun to melt. It was as if, having brought the sickness of rage and malice, it could now leave. Corum

22

rushed about in it one day, slashing at it with his naked sword and cursing it, blaming it for their ills.

But Jhary was sure now that the snow had merely been a natural occurrence, a coincidence. He ran out to try to pacify his friend. He succeeded in making Corum lower his sword and sheath it. They stood shivering in the morning light, both half-clad.

"And what of the shape on the hill?" Corum panted. "Was that coincidence, my friend?"

"It could have been. I have a feeling that all these things happened at the same time because, perhaps, something else happened. These are hints. Do you understand me?"

Corum shrugged and wrenched his arm away from Jhary's grasp. "A larger event? Is that what you mean?"

"Aye. A larger event."

"Is not what is happening to us already sufficiently unpleasant?"

"Aye. It is."

Corum saw that his friend was humouring him. He tried to smile. A sense of exhaustion filled him. All his energy was going to battle his own terrible desires. He wiped his brow with the back of his right hand.

"There must be something which can help us. I fear — I fear ..."

"We all fear, Prince Corum."

"I fear I'll slay Rhalina one night. I do, Jhary."

"We had best take to living apart, locking ourselves in our rooms. The retainers also are suffering as badly as we."

"I have noticed."

"They, too, must be separated. Shall I tell them?"

Corum fingered the pommel of his sword and his red-rimmed left eye had a wide, staring look. "Aye," he said absently. "Tell them."

"And you will do the same, Corum? I am even now trying to concoct a potion — something which will calm us and make sure we do not harm each other. Doubtless it will make us less alert, but that is better than killing ourselves."

"Killing? Aye." Corum stared at Jhary. The dandy's silk jerkin offended him, though not long since he had thought he admired it. And the man's face had an expression on it. What was it? Mocking? Why was Jhary mocking him?

"Why do you —?" He broke off, realising that he was once

23

again possessed. "We must leave Castle Erorn," he said. "Perhaps some — some ghost inhabits it now. Some evil force left behind by Glandyth. That is possible Jhary, for I have heard of such things."

Jhary looked sceptical.

"It is a possibility!" Corum yelled. Why was Jhary so stupid sometimes?

"A possibility." Jhary rubbed at his forehead and pinched the bridge of his nose. His eyes, too, were rimmed red and had a tendency to stare wildly this way and that. "A possibility, aye. But we must leave here. You are right. We must see if only Castle Erorn is affected. We must see if anywhere else suffers what we suffer. If we can get the Sky Ship from the courtyard ... The snow has melted from it now ... We must go to ... I must ..." He stopped himself. "I'm babbling now. It's the weariness. But we must seek out a friend — Prince Yurette, perhaps — ask him if he has felt the same impulses."

"You proposed that yesterday," Corum reminded him.

"And we agreed, did we not?"

"Aye." Corum began to stumble back towards the castle gate. "We agreed. And we agreed the day before yesterday, also."

"We must make preparations. Will Rhalina stay here or come with us?"

"Why do you ask? It is impertinent ..." Again Corum controlled himself. "Forgive me, Jhary."

"I do."

"What force is it that could possess us so? Turn old friends against each other? Make me desire, sometimes, to slay the woman I love most in the world?"

"We shall never discover that if we remain here," Jhary told him rather sharply.

"Very well, then," Corum said. "We'll take the air boat. We'll seek Prince Yurette. Do you feel strong enough to fly the craft?"

"I'll find the strength."

The world turned grey as the snow continued to melt. All the trees seemed grey and the hills seemed grey and the grass seemed grey. Even Castle Erorn's marvellously tinted towers took on a grey appearance and the walls within were also grey.

In the late afternoon, before sunset, Rhalina called for

Corum and for Jhary. "Come," she shouted. "Sky Ships approach us. They are behaving strangely."

They gathered at one of the windows facing the sea.

In the distance two of the beautiful metallic Sky Ships were wheeling and diving as if in a complicated dance, skimming close to the grey ocean and then hurling themselves upward at great speed. It seemed that each was attempting to get behind the other.

Something glittered.

Rhalina gasped.

"They are using those weapons — those fearful weapons with which they destroyed King Lyr and his army! They are fighting, Corum!"

"Aye," he said grimly. "They are fighting."

One of the ships suddenly staggered in the air and seemed to come to a complete stop. Then it turned over and they saw tiny figures falling from it. It righted itself. It drove upwards at the other craft, trying to ram it, but the craft managed to dodge just in time and the damaged craft continued on its course, rising higher and higher into the grey sky until it was only a shadow among the clouds.

It came back, diving at its enemy which, this time, was struck in its stern and began to spiral down towards the sea. The other ship plunged straight into the ocean and disappeared. There was a little foam on the sea where it had entered.

The remaining Sky Ship corrected its own fall and began to limp through the sky towards the land, making for the cliff across the bay from Castle Erorn, changing course in a jerky movement and heading straight for the castle.

"Does he mean to strike us?" Jhary asked.

Corum shrugged. He had come to see Castle Erorn as a haunted prison rather than as his ancient home.

If the Sky Ship smashed into Erorn's towers it would almost be as if it smashed into his own skull, driving the terrifying fury from his brain.

But the craft turned aside at the last minute and began to circle to land on the grey sward just beyond the gates.

It landed badly and Corum saw a wisp of smoke rise from its stern and curl sluggishly in the air. Men began to clamber from the ship. They were undoubtably Vadhagh, tall men with flowing cloaks and mail byrnies of gold or silver, conical helms on their heads, slender swords in their hands. They marched through the slush towards the castle.

Corum was the first to recognise the man who led them. "It is Bwydyth! Bwydyth-a-Horn! He must need our help. Come, let us greet him."

Jhary was more reluctant, but he said nothing as he followed Corum and Rhalina to the gates.

Bwydyth and his men were already ascending the path up the hill towards the gates when Corum opened them himself and stepped out, calling their friend's name.

"Greetings, Bwydyth! You are welcome here to Castle Erorn."

Bwydyth-a-Horn made no answer, but continued to march up the hill.

All at once Corum Jhaelen Irsei felt suspicion well in him. He dismissed it. The effect of the shadow lurking in his brain. He smiled and spread his arms wide.

"Bwydyth! It is I — Corum."

Jhary muttered: "Best ready yourself to draw your sword. Rhalina — you had best go inside."

She gave him a statled look. "Why? It is Bwydyth. Not an enemy."

He merely stared at her for a moment. She lowered her eyes and did as he suggested.

Corum fought against the anger within him. He breathed hard. "If Bwydyth means to fight, then he will find ..."

"Corum!" Jhary said urgently. "Keep your head clear. It is possible that we can reason with Bwydyth, for I suspect he suffers from what we have been suffering from." He called out. "Bwydyth, old friend. We are not your enemies. Come, enjoy the peace of Castle Erorn. There's no need for strifing here. We have all known these sudden furies and we must gather to discuss their nature and their cause, decide how best to discover their source."

But Bwydyth marched on up the hill towards them, and his men, grim-faced and pale, marched on behind him. Their cloaks curled in the thin breeze which had begun to blow, the steel of their swords did not shine but was as grey as the landscape.

"Bwydyth!" It was Rhalina crying from behind them. "Do not give in to that which has seized your mind. Do not fight with Corum. He is your friend. Corum found the means to bring you back to your homeland."

Bwydyth stopped. His men stopped. Bwydyth glared up at them. "Is that another thing I must hate you for, Corum?"

"Another thing? What else do you hate me for, Bwydyth?"

"Why for — for your dreadful deformities. You are unsightly. For your alliance with demons. For your choice of women and your choice of friends. For your cowardice."

"Cowardice, eh?" Jhary growled and reached for his own sword.

Corum stopped him. "Bwydyth, we know that a sickness of the mind has come upon us. It makes us hate those who love, seek to kill those whom we most desire to live. Plainly this sickness is on you as it is on us, but if we give in to it, we give in to whatever it is which wants us to destroy each other. This suggests a common enemy — something we must seek out and slay."

Bwydyth frowned, lowering his sword. "Aye. I have thought the same. Sometimes I have wondered why the fighting has started everywhere. Perhaps you are right, Corum. Aye, we will talk." He began to turn to address his company. "Men, we will ..."

One of the nearest swordsmen lunged forward with a snarl of hatred. "Fool! I knew you for a fool! You are proven a fool! You die for your foolishness." The sword passed through the byrnie and buried itself in Bwydyth's body. He cried out, groaned, tried to stagger towards his friends and then fell face down in the melting snow.

"So the poison is acting swiftly," said Jhary.

Already another man had fallen on the swordsman who had struck Bwydyth down. Two more were slain in almost as many heartbeats. Cries of rage and hatred burst from the lips of the rest. Blood spurted in the grey evening light.

The civilised folk of Gwlās-cor-Gwrys were butchering each other without reason. They were fighting amongst themselves like so many carrion dogs over a carcass.

The Third Chapter

CHAOS RETURNED

Soon the winding path to the castle was strewn with corpses. Four were left on their feet when something seemed to seize their heads and turn them to glare with blazing eyes at Corum and Jhary who still stood by the gates. The four began to move up the hill again. Corum and Jhary readied their swords.

Corum felt the anger rising in his own head, shaking his body with its intensity. It was a relief at last to be able to vent it. With a chilling yell he rushed down the hill towards the attackers, his bright sword raised, Jhary behind him.

One of the swordsmen went down before Corum's first thrust. These men were gaunt-faced and exhausted. It looked as if they had not slept for many days. Normally Corum would have known pity for them, would have tried to disarm them or merely wound them. But his own rage made him strike to kill.

And soon they were all dead.

And Corum Jhaelen Irsei stood over their corpses and panted like a mad wolf, the blood dripping from his blade into the grey ground. He stood thus for some moments until a small sound reached his ears. He turned. Jhary-a-Conel was already kneeling beside the man who had made the sound. It was Bwydyth-a-Horn and he was not quite dead.

"Corum ..." Jhary looked up at his friend. "He is calling your name, Corum."

His fury abated for the moment, Corum went to Bwydyth's side. "Aye, friend," he murmured gently.

"I tried, Corum, to fight what was inside my skull. I tried for many days, but eventually it defeated me. I am sorry, Corum ..."

"We have all suffered the sickness."

"When rational I decided to come to you in the hope that you would know of a cure. At least, I thought, I could warn you ..."

28

"And that is why your Sky Ship came to be in these parts, eh?"

"Aye. But we were followed. There was a battle and it brought back all my rage again. The whole Vadhagh race is at war, Corum — and Lywm-an-Esh is no better ... Strife governs all ..." Bwydyth's voice grew still fainter.

"Do you know why, Bwydyth?"

"No ... Prince Yurette hoped to discover ... He, too, was overcome by the berserk fury ... He — died ... Reason is banished ... We are in the grip of demons ... Chaos is returned ... We should have remained in our city ..."

Corum nodded. "It is Chaos work, without doubt. We became complacent too quickly, we ceased to be wary — and Chaos struck. But it cannot be Mabelode, for if he came to our plane he would be destroyed as Xiombarg was destroyed. He must be working through an agency. But who?"

"Glandyth?" whispered Jhary. "Could it be the Earl of Krae? All Chaos needs is one willing to serve it. If the will exists, the power is given."

Bwydyth-a-Horn began to cough. "Ah, Corum, forgive me for this ..."

"There is naught to forgive, since we are equally possessed by something which is beyond our power to fight."

"Find what it is, Corum ..." Bwydyth's eyes burned near-black as he raised himself on one elbow. "Destroy it if you can ... Revenge me ... revenge us all ..."

And Bwydyth died.

Corum was trembling with emotion. "Jhary — have you manufactured the potion of which you spoke?"

"It is almost ready, though I make no claims for it yet. It might not counter the madness."

"Be quick."

Corum rose to his feet and walked back to the castle, sheathing his sword.

As he entered the gates he heard a scream and went running through the grey galleries until he entered a room of bright fountains. There was Rhalina beating off the attack of two of the female retainers. The women were shrieking like beasts and striking at her with their nails. Corum drew his sword again, reversed it, struck the nearest woman on the base of the skull. She went down and the other whirled, foaming at the mouth. Corum leapt forward and with his jewelled hand struck her on the jaw. She, too, fell.

Corum felt rage rising in him again. He glared at the weeping Rhalina. "What did you do to offend them?"

She looked at him in astonishment. "I? Nothing, Corum. Corum! I did nothing!"

"Then why —?" He realised his voice was harsh, shrill. Deliberately he took control of himself. "I am sorry, Rhalina. I understand. Ready yourself for a journey. We leave in our Sky Ship as soon as possible. Jhary may have a medicine which will calm us. We must go to Lywm-an-Esh to see if there is any hope there. We must try to contact Lord Arkyn and hope the Lord of Law will help us."

"Why is he not already helping us?" she asked bitterly. "We helped him regain his Realm and now, it seems, he abandons us to Chaos."

"If Chaos is active here, then it is active elsewhere. It could be that there are worse dangers in his Realm, or in the Realm of his brother Lord of Law. You know that none of the gods may interfere directly in mortal affairs."

"But Chaos tries more frequently," she said.

"That is the nature of Chaos and that is why mortals are best served by Law, for Law believes in the freedom of mortals and Chaos sees us merely as playthings to be moulded and used according to its whims. Quickly, now, prepare to leave."

"But it is hopeless, Corum. Chaos must be so much more powerful than Law. We have done all we can to fight it. Why not admit that we are doomed?"

"Chaos only seems more powerful because it is aggressive and willing to use any means to gain its end. Law endures. Make no mistake, I do not like the role in which Fate has cast me — I would that someone else had my burden — but the power of Law must be preserved if possible. Now go — hurry."

She went away reluctantly while Corum made sure that the retainers were not badly hurt. He did not like to leave them, for he was sure that they would turn upon each other soon. He decided that he would leave them some of the potion Jhary was preparing and hope that it would last them.

He frowned. Could Glandyth really be the cause of this? But Glandyth was no sorcerer — he was a brute, a bloody-handed warrior, a good tactician and, in his own terms, had many virtues, but he had little subtlety or even desire to use sorcery, for he feared it.

Yet there were no others left in this Realm who would willingly make themselves servants of Chaos — and one had to be willing or Chaos could not gain entry to the Realm at all ...

Corum decided to wait until he discovered more before continuing to speculate. If he could reach Halwyg-nan-Vake and the Temple of Law, he might be able to contact Lord Arkyn and seek his advice.

He went to the room where he kept his arms and armour and he drew on his silver byrnie, his silver greaves and his conical silver helm with the three characters set into it over the peak — characters which stood for his full name. And over all this he put his scarlet robe. Then he selected weapons — a bow, arrows and a lance, a war-axe of exquisitive workmanship — and he buckled on his long, strong sword. Once again he garbed himself for war and he made both a magnificent and a terrible figure, with his glittering six-fingered hand and the jewelled patch which covered the jewelled Eye of Rhynn. He had prayed that he would never have to dress himself thus again, that he would never have to use the alien hand grafted to his left wrist or peer through the eye into the fearsome netherworld to summon the living dead to his aid. Yet in his heart he had known that the power of Chaos had not been vanquished, that the worst was still to come.

He felt weary, however, for his battle with the madness in his skull was as exhausting as any physical fight.

Jhary came in and he, too, was dressed for travelling, though he disdained armour, wearing a quilted leather jerkin, stamped with designs in gold and platinum, in lieu of a breastplate — his only concession. His wide-brimmed hat was placed at a jaunty angle on his head, his long hair was brushed so that it shone and arranged on his shoulders. He wore flamboyant silks and satins, elaborately decorated boots trimmed with red and white lace, and was the very picture of effete dandyism. Only the soldier's sword at his belt denied the impression. On his shoulder was the small black and white winged cat which was his constant companion. In his hand he held a bottle with a thin neck. A brownish liquid swirled inside.

"It is made." He spoke slowly, as if in a trance. "And it has the desired effect, I think. It has driven away my fury, though

31

I feel drowsy. Some of the drowsiness should wear off. I hope it does."

Corum looked at him suspiciously. "It might counter the fury — but we shall be slow to defend ourselves if attacked. It slows the wits, Jhary!"

"It offers a different perspective, I grant you." Jhary smiled a dreamy smile. "But it's our only chance, Corum. And, speaking for myself, I would rather die in peace than in mental anquish."

"I'll grant you that." Corum accepted the bottle. "How much shall I take?"

"It is strong. Just a little on the tip of the forefinger."

Corum tilted the bottle and got a small amount of the potion on his finger. Cautiously he licked it. He gave Jhary back the bottle. "I feel no different. Perhaps it does not work on the Vadhagh metabolism."

"Perhaps. Now you must give some to Rhalina ..."

"And the servants."

"Aye — fair enough — the servants ..."

They stood in the courtyard brushing the last of the snow off the canopy covering the Sky Ship, peeling back the cloth to reveal the rich blues, greens and yellows of the metallic hull. Jhary clambered slowly in and began to pass his hands over the variously coloured crystals on the panel in the prow. This was not as large a Sky Ship as the first they had encountered. This one was open to the elements when not utilising the protective power of is invisible energy screen. A whisper of sound came from the ship and it lifted an inch off the ground. Corum helped Rhalina in and then he, too, was aboard, lying on one of the couches and watching Jhary as he prepared the craft for flight.

Jhary moved slowly, a slight smile on his face. Corum, full of a sense of well-being, watched him. He looked over to the couch where Rhalina had placed herself and he saw that she was almost asleep. The potion was working well in that the sense of fury had disappeared. But part of Corum still knew that his present euphoria might be as dangerous as his earlier rage. He knew that he had exchanged one madness for another, in some senses.

He hoped that another Sky Ship would not attack them, as Bwydyth's had been attacked, for, apart from their present disability, they were all unfamiliar with the art of aerial war-

32

fare. It was the best Jhary could do to pilot the Sky Ship in the desired direction.

At last the craft lifted gently into the cold, grey air, turning west and moving along the coast towards Lywm-an-Esh.

And as the ship drifted on its way Corum looked down at the world, all bleak and frozen, and wondered if spring would ever come again to Bro-an-Vadhagh.

He opened his lips to speak to Jhary, but the dandy was absorbed with the controls. He watched as, suddenly, the little black and white cat sprang from Jhary's shoulder, clung for a moment to the side of the Sky Ship and then flew off over the land, to disappear behind a line of hills.

For a moment Corum wondered why the cat had deserted them, but then he forgot about it as he once again became interested in the sea and the landscape below.

The Fourth Chapter

A NEW ALLY FOR EARL GLANDYTH

The little cat flew steadily throughout the day, changing its direction constantly as if it followed an invisible and winding path through the sky. Soon it had ceased to fly inland, hesitated, then headed out over the cliffs and over the sea, which it hated. Islands came in sight.

They were the Nhadragh Isles where lived the remainder of the folk who had become grovelling slaves of the Mabden in order to preserve their lives. Though presently released from that slavery, they had become so degenerate that their race might still die from apathy, for most could not even hate the Vadhagh now.

The cat was searching for something, following a psychic rather than a physical scent; a scent which only he could distinguish.

Once before had the little winged cat followed a similar scent, when he had gone to Kalenwyr to witness the great massing of Mabden and the summoning of their now banished gods the Dog and the Horned Bear. This time, however, the cat was acting upon its own impulses, it had not been sent to the Nhadragh Isles by Jhary-a-Conel its master.

In what was almost the exact centre of the group of green islands was the largest of them, called Maliful by the Nhadragh. Like all the islands it contained many ruins — ruins of towns, ruins of castles, ruins of villages. Some were ruins thanks to the passage of time, but others were ruins thanks to the passage of Mabden armies when they had attacked the Nhadragh Isles at the height of King Lyr-a-Brodes power. It had been Earl Glandyth and his Denledhyssi Chariot-warriors who had led these expeditions, just as, later, he had led expeditions to the Vadhagh castles and destroyed what was left of the Vadhagh race, save Corum — or so he had thought. The destruction of the two elder races — the Shefanhow as Glandyth called them — had taken a matter of a few years. They had been completely unprepared for Mabden attack, had not been able to believe in the power of creatures scarcely more intelligent or cultured than other beasts. So they had died.

And only a few Nadragh had been spared — used like dogs to hunt down their fellows, to search for their ancient Vadhagh enemies, to see into other dimensions and tell their masters what they perceived. These had been the least brave of their race — those who preferred degenerate slavery to death.

The little cat saw some of their camps amongst the ruins of the towns. They had been returned here after the Battle of Halwyg, when their Mabden masters had been defeated. They had made no attempt to rebuild their castles or cities, but lived like primitives, many of them unaware that the ruins had once been buildings created by their own kind. They were dressed in iron and fur, after the manner of the Nhadragh. They had dark, flat features and the hair of their heads grew down to meet bushy eyebrows sprouting above deep sockets. They were thick-set people, heavily muscled and strong. Once they had been as powerful and as civilised as the Vadhagh but the Vadhagh decline had not come so swiftly as theirs.

Now the broken towers of Os, once the capital of Maliful and the whole Nhadragh lands, came in sight. Os the Beautiful the city had been called by its inhabitants, but it was beautiful no longer. Broken walls were festooned with weeds, towers were stretched upon the ground, houses gave shelter to rats and weasels and other vermin, but not to Nhadragh.

The cat continued to follow the psychic scent. It circled

over a squat building which was still intact. Upon the flat roof of the building a dome had been built. The dome was transparent and it glowed. Within two figures could be seen, black against the yellow light. One figure was burly, armoured, and the other was shorter, dressed in furs, but wider than its companion. Muffled voices came from within the dome. The cat landed on the roof, stalked towards the dome, flattened its little head against the transparent material and, its eyes wide, watched and listened.

Glandyth-a-Krae frowned as he peered over Ertil's shoulder into the billowing smoke and the boiling liquid below. "Does the spell continue to work, Ertil?"

The Nhadragh nodded his head. "They still battle amongst themselves. Never has my sorcery worked so well."

"That is because the powers of Chaos aid you, fool! Or aid me, I should say, for it it I who am pledged, body and soul, to the Lords of Chaos." He glanced around the littered dome. It was full of dead animals, bunches of herbs, bottles of dust and liquids. Some rats and monkeys sat apathetically in cages along one wall, a shelf of scrolls below them. Once Ertil's father had been a wise scholar and he had tought Ertil much. But Ertil was evolving as the other Nhadragh evolved. He translated the wisdom into sorcery, superstition. But the wisdom itself was still powerful, as Earl Glandyth-a-Krae, picking now at his yellow fangs, had discovered.

Earl Glandyth's red, acned face was half-hidden by his huge beard which had been braided and laced with ribbons, just as his long, black hair was braided. His grey eyes hinted at an inner disease, just as his fat, red lips suggested corrupted offal. Earl Glandyth snarled. "What of Prince Corum? And the others who befriended him? What of all the Shefanhow who came from the magic city?"

"I cannot see what befalls individuals, my lord," whined the sorcerer. "I only know the spell is working."

"I hope you speak truly, sorcerer."

"I do, my lord. Was it not a spell given us by the powers of Chaos? The Cloud of Contention spreads, invisible upon the wind, turning each man against his companion, against his children, his wife." A tremulous grin appeared on the Nhadragh's dark face. "The Vadhagh fall upon each other. They die. They all die."

"Aye — but does Corum die? That is what I must know.

35

That the others perish is well and good, but not so important. With Corum gone and disruption in the land I can rally supporters in Lywm-an-Esh and, with my Denledhyssi, reconquer the lands King Lyr lost. Can you not concoct a special spell for Corum, sorcerer?"

Ertil trembled. "Corum is mortal — he must suffer as the others suffer."

"He is cunning — he has powerful help — he might escape. We sail for Lywm-an-Esh tomorrow. Is there no way of telling for certain that Corum is dead or seized by the madness which seizes the others?"

"No way that I know, master."

Glandyth scratched at his pitted face with his broken fingernails. "Are you sure you do not deceive me, Shefanhow?"

"I would not, master. I would not!"

Glandyth grinned into the terrified eyes of the Nhadragh sorcerer. "I believe you, Ertil." He laughed. "Still, a little more aid from Chaos would not go amiss. Summon that demon again — the one from Mabelode's plane."

Ertil whimpered. "It takes a year off my life every time I perform such a summoning."

Glandyth drew his long knife. He placed the tip on Ertil's flat nose. "Summon it, Ertil!"

"I will summon it."

Ertil shuffled to the other side of the dome and took one of the monkeys from its cage. The creature whimpered in echo of Ertil's own whimperings. Although it looked at the Nhadragh in fear it clung to him as if for safety, finding security nowhere else in the room. Next Ertil took an X-shaped frame from a corner and he stood this in a specially made indentation in the scarred surface of the table. All the while he shuddered. All the while he moaned. And Glandyth paced impatiently, refusing to see or hear the signs of the Nhadragh sorcerer's distress.

Now Ertil gave the monkey something to sniff and the east became quiescent. Ertil positioned it against the frame and took nails and a hammer from his pouch.

Methodically, he began to crucify the monkey while it gibbered and squawked and blood ran out of the holes in its little hands and feet.

Ertil was pale and he looked as if he might vomit.

The cat's eyes widened further as it watched this barbaric ritual and it became just a trifle nervous, the hairs stiffening on the back of its neck and its tail jerking back and forth, but it continued to observe the scene in the dome.

"Hurry, you Shefanhow filth!" Glandyth growled. "Hurry, lest I seek another sorcerer!"

"You know there are no others left who would aid you or Chaos," Ertil mumbled.

"Be silent! Continue with your damned business."

Glandyth scowled. It was plain that Ertil spoke the truth. None feared the Mabden now — none save the Nhadragh who had developed the habit of fearing them.

The monkey's teeth were chattering. Its eyes rolled. Ertil heated an iron in the brazier. While the iron got hot, he traced a complicated figure around the crucified beast. Then he placed bowls in each of the ten corners and he lit what was in the bowls. He took a scroll in one hand and the white-hot iron in the other. The dome began to fill with green and yellow smoke. Glandyth coughed and took a kerchief from inside his iron-studded jerkin. He looked nervous and backed into a corner.

"Yrkoon, Yrkoon, Esel Asan. Yrkoon, Yrkoon, Nasha Fasal ..." The chant went on and on and with every verse Ertil plunged the hot iron into the writhing body of the monkey. The monkey did not die, for the iron missed its vitals, but it was plainly in dreadful agony. "Yrkoon, Yrkoon, Meshel Feran. Yrkoon, Yrkoon, Palaps Oli."

The smoke thickened and the cat could see only shadows in the room.

"Yrkoon, Yrkoon, Cenil Pordit ..."

A distant noise. It mingled with the shrieks of the tortured monkey.

A wind blowing.

The smoke cleared suddenly. The scene in the dome was as sharp as before. No longer was the monkey crucified upon the frame. Something else hung there. It had a human form but was no larger than the monkey. Its features were closer to those of the Vadhagh than the Mabden, though there was evil and malice in the tiny face.

"You summoned me again, Ertil." The voice was of the pitch and loudness of an ordinary voice. It seemed strange that it issued from such a small mouth.

"Aye — I summoned you, Yrkoon. We need help from your master Mabelode ..."

"More help?" The voice was bantering. Yrkoon smiled. "More?"

"You know that we work for him. Without us you would have no means of reaching this Realm at all."

"What of it? Why should my master Lord Mabelode be interested in your Realm?"

"You know why! He wants both the old Sword Realms back for Chaos — and he wants vengeance on Corum who was instrumental in destroying the power of his brother Arioch and his sister Xiombarg, the Knight and Queen of the Swords!"

Hanging comfortably on the frame the demon shrugged. "And so? What is it you want?"

Glandyth stepped forward, bunching his fist.

"It is what I want not what this sorcerer wants! I want power, demon! I want the means of destroying Corum — of destroying the power of Law on this plane! Give me that power, demon!"

"I have given you much power already," the demon said reasonably. "I gave you the means of creating the Cloud of Contention. Your enemies fight each other to the death. And you are still not satisfied!"

"Tell me if Corum lives!"

"I can tell you nothing. We have no means of reaching this plane unless you summon us and, as you well know, we cannot remain here for long — we can only take the place of another creature for a short while. Thus is the Balance deceived — or, if not decived, mollified."

"Give me more power, Sir Demon!"

"I cannot *give* you power. I can only tell you how to acquire it. And know this, Glandyth-a-Krae, and be warned — if you take more of the gifts of Chaos, then you will assume the attributes of all those who accept those gifts. Are you ready to become what you most profess to loathe?"

"What's that?"

Yrkoon chuckled. "A Shefanhow. A demon. I was human once ..."

Glandyth's mouth twisted and he clenched his fists. "I'll make any bargain to have my revenge on Corum and his kind!"

"And thus we shall be mutually served. Very well. Power you shall have."

"And power for my men — power for the Denledhyssi!"

"Very well. Power for them, too."

"Great, fierce power!" Glandyth's eyes were afire. "Massive power! Invincible power!"

"There is no such thing while the Balance rules. You shall have what you can carry."

"Good. I can carry much. I shall sail for the mainland, take their cities and their castles once again, while they fight amongst themselves. I will rule this whole world. Lyr and the rest were weak. But I shall be strong, with the Power of Chaos at my command!"

"Lyr, too, had aid from Chaos," Yrkoon reminded him sardonically.

"But he knew not how to use it. I begged him to give me more men to destroy Corum, but he would not give me enough. If Corum were dead, Lyr would be alive today. That is my proof."

"It must give you satisfaction," said the demon. "Now listen. I will tell you what you must do."

The Fifth Chapter

THE DESERTED CITY

The Sky Ship flew over the hill in the sea where Castle Moidel had once stood. There was no castle there now. Corum looked down on it with a sense of regret which was quickly gone, for the euphoria of the potion was still upon him. And soon they had reached the coast of Lywm-an-Esh. At first the land seemed normal, but after a while they saw small groups of riders, rarely more than three or four, rushing wildly through fields and forests, attacking any other group they came upon. Women fought women and children fought children. There were many corpses. Corum's apathy slowly changed to horror and he was glad that Rhalina slept, that Jhary had time only to look down occasionally.

"Make haste for Halwyg-nan-Vake," corum told his friend when Jhary glanced questioningly at him. "There is nothing we can do for them until we discover what causes their madness."

Jhary took the bottle from his pouch and held it up, but Corum shook his head. "No. There is not enough. Besides, how could we persuade them to take it? If we are to save any lives at all, we must attack that which attacks us."

Jhary sighed. "How do you attack a madness, Corum?"

"That we must discover. I pray that the Temple of Law still stands and that Arkyn will come to it if we attempt to summon him."

Jhary jerked his thumb downwards. "This is like the madness which touched them before."

"Only it is stronger. Before it merely nibbled at their brains. Now it eats them entirely."

"They destroy all that they rebuilt. Is there any point in —?"

"They can rebuild again. There is a point."

Jhary shrugged. "I wonder where my cat has gone," he said.

When the Sky Ship circled over Halwyg-nan-Vake and began to land near the Temple of Law Rhalina woke up. She smiled at Corum as if she had forgotten all that had recently passed. But then she frowned as if remembering a nightmare. "Corum"

"It is true," he said softly. "And we are at Halwyg now. The Floral City seems deserted. I do not know the explanation."

He had half-expected to see the beautiful city in flames. Instead, save for one or two damaged buildings and gardens, it was intact. Yet none walked its streets or patrolled its walls. The palace was unoccupied as far as he could tell.

Jhary brought the Sky Ship down as he had learned to do when, in gentler times, Bwydyth-a-Horn had taught him its secrets.

They landed in a wide, white street. Near by stood the Temple of Law, of but one storey and without ostentatious decoration. A simple building with a sign over its portal — a single straight arrow — the Arrow of Law.

They climbed from the Sky Ship on trembling legs. The combination of the flight and the potion had weakened them somewhat. They began, unsteadily, to advance up the path towards the Temple.

It was then that a figure appeared in the doorway. His clothes were torn and bloody and one eye had been gouged from his old face. He was sobbing, but his hands clawed out at them like the talons of a wounded, ferocious animal.

"It is Aleryon!" Rhalina gasped. "The priest — Aleryon-a-Nyvish! The sickness is upon him, too!"

The old man was weak and he could not resist when Corum and Jhary stepped swiftly forward and grasped him, pinning his arms to his sides while Jhary removed the stopper of his bottle with his teeth, dabbed a little of his potion on his finger and let Corum force the old man's jaws open. Jhary smeared the stuff on Aleryon's tongue. The priest tried to spit it out, his eyes rolling, his nostrils dilating like those of a horse in fever. But almost immediately he was quiet. His body went limp and he began to slide to the ground.

"Let us take him into the Temple," Corum said.

When they lifted him he offered no resistance. They carried him into the coolness of the interior and laid him on the floor.

"Corum?" croaked the priest, opening his eyes. "The Chaos fury leaves me. I am myself again — or almost so."

"What has happened to the folk of Halwyg?" Jhary asked him. "Are they all destroyed? Where have they gone?"

"They are mad. Not one was sane by yesterday. I fought the sickness as long I could …"

"But where are they, Aleryon?"

"Gone. They are off in the hills, on the plains, in the forests. They are hiding from each other — attacking each other from time to time. Not one man trusted another and so they left the city, you see …"

"Has Lord Arkyn visited your temple?" Corum asked the old priest. "Has he spoken to you?"

"Once — early on. He told me to send for you, but I could not. No one would go and I knew of no other way of reaching you, Prince Corum. And when the rage came, then I was in no state to — to receive Lord Arkyn. I could not summon him, as, traditionally, I summon him every day."

Corum helped Aleryon to his feet. "Summon him now. The whole world is possessed by Chaos. Summon him now, Aleryon!"

"I am not sure."

"You must."

41

"I will try." Aleryon's wounded face grew grim, for now he fought against the euphoria of Jhary's potion. "I will try."

And he tried. He tried for all the rest of that afternoon, his voice growing hoarse as he chanted the ritual prayer to Law. For many years that prayer had gone unanswered, while Law was banished and Arioch ruled in the name of Chaos. But recently the prayer had sometimes summoned the great Lord of Law.

Now there was no answer.

Aleryon paused at last. "He does not hear. Or, if he hears, he cannot come. Is Chaos returned in all her power, Corum?"

Corum Jhaelen Irsei looked at the floor and slowly shook his head. "Perhaps."

"Look!" said Rhalina, pushing her long black hair away from her face. "Jhary, it is your cat."

The little black and white cat flew through the door and settled on Jhary's shoulder. It nuzzled his ear, a series of low sounds coming from its throat. Jhary looked surprised and then became intent, listening closely to the cat.

"It speaks to him!" Aleryon murmured in astonishment. "The creature speaks!"

"It communicates," Jhary told him, "yes."

At length the cat became quiet and, balancing on Jhary's shoulder still, began to wash itself.

"What did it tell you?" Corum asked.

"It told me of Glandyth-a-Krae."

"So — he does live!"

"Not only does he live but he appears to have made a pact with King Mabelode of Chaos — through the medium of a treacherous Nhadragh sorcerer. And Chaos told him of the spell which is now upon us. And Chaos has promised him yet greater power."

"Where is Glandyth?"

"On Maliful — in Os."

"We must go there, find Glandyth, destroy him."

"No point. Glandyth comes to us."

"By sea? There is still time."

"Across the sea. He and his men have some Chaos beasts at their command — things which the cat could not describe. Even now he flies for Lywm-an-Esh — and he is seeking us, Corum."

"We shall be here and we shall fight him at long last."

Jhary looked sceptical. "The two of us — drugged so that our reactions are slow and our sense of survival low?"

"We will find others — administer your potion ..." Corum stopped. He knew that it was impossible — that even under normal conditions he would be hard put to fight the Denledhyssi, even with the aid ... His face cleared and then grew dark again. "Perhaps it can be done, Jhary, if I make use of the Hand of Kwll and the Eye of Thynn once more."

Jhary-a-Conel shrugged. "We must hope so, for there is naught else we can do. If only we could find Tanelorn, as I wanted to do before. I am sure we should find help there. But I have no clue as to its current whereabouts."

"You speak of the mythical city of tranquility — Eternal Tanelorn?" said Aleryon. "You know it exists?"

Jhary smiled. "If I have a home — then that home is Tanelorn. It exists in every age, at every time, on every plane — but it is sometimes hard to find."

"Can we not search the planes in the Sky Ship?" Rhalina said. "For the Sky Ship can travel between the Realms as we know."

"My knowledge does not extend to guiding it through those strange dimensions," Jhary told them. "Bwydyth told me something of how to make it travel through the walls between the Realms, but I know nothing of steering it. No, we must hope to find Tanelorn on this plane, if we are to find it at all. But in the meantime we must think more of Glandyth and escaping him."

"Or doing battle with him," Corum said. "We might have the means of defeating him."

"We might, aye."

"You must go to watch for him," Aleryon said. "I will stay here with the Lady Rhalina. Together we shall continue to try summoning Lord Arkyn."

Corum nodded his agreement. "You are a brave old man, priest. I thank you."

Outside in the silent streets Corum and Jhary walked listlessly towards the centre of the city. Time upon time Corum would raise his alien left hand and inspect it. Time upon time he would lower it and then touch his jewelled eye-patch with his right hand. Then he would glance up into the sky through his one mortal eye, his silver helm glinting in the sunlight, for the clouds had cleared and it was a calm winter's day.

Neither man could express his thoughts. They were thoughts both profound and desperate. It seemed that the end had come when they had least expected it. Somehow Law had been vanquished, Chaos had regained all its old strength — perhaps was stronger. And they had not, until a short time before, had any hint of it. They felt confused, betrayed, doomed, impotent.

The dead city seemed to symbolise the emptiness in their own souls. They hoped that they would see an inhabitant — just one human being, even if he attacked them.

The flowers blew gently in the breeze, but instead of signifying peace, they signified an ominous calm.

Glandyth was coming from the sky, his strength reinforced by the power of Chaos.

It was with hardly any emotion at all that Corum eventually noticed them. Black shadows flying from the East — a score of them. He indicated them to Jhary.

"We had best return to the Temple and warn Aleryon and Rhalina."

Would not they be safest in the Temple of Law?"

"I think not — not now, Jhary."

Black shadows flying from the East. Flying low. Flying purposefully. Huge wings beating, strange cries sounding in the evening air, cries which were fierce and yet full of melancholy, the cries of damned souls. Yet these were beasts. Long- necked beasts, whose heads writhed at the end of their stalks, staring this way and that, scanning the ground as hawks might scan for prey. Long, thin heads with long, thin fangs projecting from their red mouths. Blank, miserable eyes. Despairing voices, cawing as if pleading for release. And on their black, broad backs were strapped the wheelless chariots of the Denledhyssi, and in these hastily fashioned howdahs were the Mabden murderers themselves, and in the leading one stood a figure in a horned helm with a great iron sword in his hand. And they thought they could hear his laughter, though it must be another sound, perhaps a sound from the monstrous black flying things.

"It is Glandyth of course," said Corum. A crooked smile was on his face. "Well, we must try to fight him. If I can summon aid, it can engage Glandyth and his things while we run to warn Rhalina."

He raised his good right hand to his bad right eye, to pull back the patch and let himself see into the netherworld where waited those whom he had slain with the power of the Hand of Kwll and the Eye of Rhynn, who were now his prisoners, waiting to be released to take other foes who might replace them and so free them from that netherworld for good. But the patch would not move, it was as if it was glued to the eye beneath. He pulled with all his strength. He raised the Hand of Kwll with its supernatural strength to pull back the patch, but the Hand of Kwll refused to approach the patch. Those things which had aided him now plainly refused to aid him.

Was the power of Chaos so great that it could control even these?

With a sob Corum turned and began to run through the streets, back towards the Temple of Law.

The Sixth Chapter

THE WEARY GOD

And when Corum and Jhary came to the Temple of Law with horror in their hearts they saw that Rhalina was waiting for them and she was smiling.

"He is here! He has come!" she cried. "It is Lord Arkyn …"

"And Glandyth comes from the East," panted Jhary. "We must flee in the Sky Ship. It is all we can do. Corum's power is gone — neither the Hand nor the Eye will obey him."

Corum strode into the Temple. He was resentful and wished to express his resentment to Arkyn of Law whom he had helped and who was not now helping him.

There was something hovering at the far end of the Temple, close to where a pale Aleryon sat with his back against the wall. A face? A body? Corum peered hard, but his peering seemed to make it fainter.

"Lord Arkyn?"

A far away voice: *"Aye …"*

"What is the matter? Why are the forces of Law so weak?"

"They are stretched so thinly through the two Realms which we control. Mabelode sends all his forces to aid those

45

who serve Chaos here ... *We fight on ten planes, Corum ...
ten planes ... and we are so recently established ... our power
is still weak ...*"

Corum held up his useless, alien hand. "Why do I no
longer control the Eye of Rhynn and the Hand of Kwll? It
was our one hope of defeating Glandyth who even now comes
against us!

*"I know that ... You must escape ... take your Sky Ship
through the dimensions ... seek Eternal Tanelorn ... there is
a correspondence between your powerlessness and your need
to find Tanelorn ..."*

"A correspondence? What correspondence?"

*"I can only sense it ... I am weakened by this struggle,
Corum ... I am weary ... My powers are thin now ... Find
Tanelorn ..."*

"How can I? Jhary cannot steer the Sky Ship through the
dimensions."

"He must try to do so ..."

"Lord Arkyn — you must give me clearer instructions.
Even now Glandyth comes to Halwyg. He intends to seize this
whole plane and rule it. He intends to destroy all of us who
remain. How can we defend those who suffer the Chaos madness?"

*"Tanelorn ... Seek Tanelorn ... It is the only way you can
hope to save them ... I can tell you no more ... It is all I see
... all I see ..."*

"You are a feeble god, Lord Arkyn. Perhaps I should have
pledged my loyalty to Chaos, for if horror and death are to
rule the world, one might as well become that horror and that
death ..."

*"Do not be bitter, Corum ... There is still some hope that
you may succeed in banishing Chaos from all the Fifteen
Planes ..."*

"It is strength I need now — not hope."

*"Hope to find the strength you need in Tanelorn. Farewell
..."*

And the vague shape vanished. Outside Corum heard the
cries of the black flying things. He went to where Aleryon
lay. The old man had exhausted himself trying to call Arkyn.
"Come, old man. We will take you to the Sky Ship with us —
if there is time."

But Aleryon did not reply for, while Corum had conversed
with the weary god, he had died.

46

Rhalina and Jhary-a-Conel were already standing by the Sky Ship, staring upwards as the great black beasts began to descend on Halwyg.

"I spoke to Arkyn," Corum told them. "He was of little help. He said we must escape through the dimensions and seek Tanelorn. I told him that you could not guide the craft beyond this plane. He said that we must."

Jhary shrugged and helped Rhalina aboard. "Then we must. Or, at least, we must try."

"If only we could rally defenders from the City in the Pyramid. Their weapons would destroy even Glandyth's Chaos allies."

"But they destroy each other with them. This is what Glandyth knew."

They stood all three in the Sky Ship as Jhary passed his hands over the crystals and brought them to life. The craft began to rise. Jhary pointed its prow towards the West, away from Glandyth.

But Glandyth had seen them now. The black wings beat louder and the cries increased in volume. The Denledhyssi began to sweep down towards the only three mortals in the world who were aware of what had happened to them.

Jhary bit his lip as he studied the crystals. "It is a question of making accurate passes over these things," he said. "I am striving to remember what Bwydyth taught me."

The Sky Ship was moving swiftly now, but their pursuers kept pace with them. The long necks of the flying beasts were poised like snakes about to strike. Red mouths stretched wide. Fangs flashed.

Something foul streamed from those mouths like oily black smoke. Like the tongues of lizards they shot towards the Sky Ship. Desperately Jhary turned the craft this way and that, attempting to avoid the tendrils. One curled around the stern and the ship stopped moving for a moment before it broke free. Rhalina clung to Corum. Uselessly, he had drawn his sword.

The little black and white cat clung with all its claws to Jhary's shoulder. It had recognised Glandyth and its eyes had widened in something akin to fear.

Now Corum heard a yell and he knew that Glandyth realised who it was trying to escape from Halwyg. Although the barbarian was a good distance away, Corum thought he felt

Glandyth's eyes glaring into his own. He stared back with his one human eye, the sword raised to protect himself and Rhalina, and he saw that Glandyth, too, brandished his great iron broadsword, almost as if challenging him to single combat. The flying serpents hissed and cackled and sent from their throats more of the smoky tendrils.

Four of the things coiled around the ship. Jhary attempted to increase the speed.

"We can go no faster! We are trapped!"

"Then you must try to move through the planes. We might escape them that way."

"Those are Chaos creatures. It is likely they too can cross the walls between the Realms!"

Hopelessly Corum hacked at the tendrils with his blade, but it was as if he cut through smoke. Inexorably they were being pulled back to where the Denledhyssi hovered, triumphantly waiting for them to be drawn close enough so that they could board the Sky Ship and slay its occupants.

Then the black wings grew hazy and Corum saw that the city below was beginning to fade. Lightning seemed to flicker through sudden darkness. Globes of purple light appeared. The boat shuddered like a frightened deer and Corum felt a familiar nausea sieze him. Furiously the black wings beat as they became clearer. He had guessed rightly, had Jhary. The creatures were able to follow them through the dimensions.

Jhary made more passes over the instruments. The boat rocked and threatened to turn over. Again came the peculiar sensations, the vibrations, the lightnings and globes of golden flame in a rushing, turbulent cloud of red and orange.

The tongues of smoke which restrained them disappeared. The black creatures still flew on, sighted through the zig-zags of utter darkness and blinding brightness. Their voices could still be heard, as also could be heard the roaring rage of Glandyth-a-Krae.

And then there was silence.

Corum could not see Rhalina. He could not see Jhary. He could only feel the boat still beneath his feet.

They were drifting in total blackness and absolute silence, neither in one dimension nor another.

BOOK TWO

*In which Prince Corum and his companions learn the full
import of what Chaos is and what it intends to become and
discover something more concerning the nature of time and
identity.*

The First Chapter

CHAOS UNBOUNDED

"Corum?"

It was Rhalina's voice.

"Corum?"

"I am here."

He stretched out his right hand and tried to touch her. At last he felt her hair beneath his fingers. He encircled her shoulders with his arm.

"Jhary?" he said. "Are you there?"

"I am here. I am trying different configurations, but the crystals do not respond. Is this Limbo, Corum?"

"I assume so. If it were not that we can breathe and it is relatively warm, I would think the Sky Ship adrift in the cosmos, beyond the sky."

Silence.

And then a thin line of golden light could be seen, cutting across the blackness as if dividing it in two, rather like a horizon, or the crack of light from beneath a gigantic door. And while they remained in the blackness the area of blackness above the golden line began, it seemed, to move upwards, like a curtain in a vast theatre.

And now, though they could still not see each other, they saw the wide area of gold, saw it begin to change.

"What is it, Corum?"

"I know not, Rhalina. Jhary?"

"This limbo might be the domain of the Cosmic Balance —— a neutral territory, as it were, where no gods or mortals come in ordinary circumstances."

"Have we drifted into it by accident?"

"I do not know."

This is what they saw then:

All was huge, but in proportion. A rider spurring his horse across a desert beneath a white and purple sky. The rider had milk-white hair and it streamed behind him. His eyes were red and full of wild bitterness, his skin was bone-white. Physically he somewhat resembled the Vadhagh, for he had the same unhuman face. He was an albino, clothed all in black, baroque armour, every part of it covered in fine, detailed metal-work, a huge helm upon his head, a black sword at his side.

And now the rider was no longer upon a horse. He rode a beast that somewhat resembled those which had pursued them — a flying beast — a dragon. The black sword was in his hand and it gave off a strange, black radiance. The rider rode the dragon as if it were a horse, seated in a saddle, his feet in stirrups, but he was strapped to the saddle to save him falling. He was crying out.

And below him there were other dragons, evidently brothers to the one he rode. They were engaged in aerial battles with misshapen things with the jaws of whales. A green mist drifted across the scene and obscured it.

Now they saw the assymetrical outlines of a gigantic castle, flowing upwards to form its shape even as they watched. Battlements, turrets, towers all appeared. The dragon-rider ordered his beasts towards it and they released flaming venom from their mouths, directing it at the castle. A few others who followed the rider also sat upon the backs of the dragons.

They passed the blazing castle and came now to an undulating plain. Upon this plain stood all the demons and corrupt, warped things of Chaos, arranged as if for battle. And here, too, were gods — Dukes of Hell every one — Malohin, Xiombarg, Zhortra and more — Chardros the Reaper, with monstrous, hairless head and sweeping scythe — and the oldest of the gods, Slortar the Old, slender and lovely as a youth of sixteen.

And it was this massed might that the dragon-riders attacked.

Surely they must perish.

Fiery venom splashed across the scene and again there was only golden light.

"What did we see?" Corum whispered. "Do you know, Jhary?"

"Aye. I know. I have been there — or will be there. We see another age, another plane. The mightiest battle between Law and Chaos, Gods and Mortals, that I have ever witnessed. The white-faced one I served in a different guise. He is called Elric of Melnibone."

"You mentioned him once, when we first met."

"He is, like you, a champion chosen by destiny to fight so that the equilibrium of the Cosmic Balance might be preserved." Jhary's voice sounded sad. "I remember his friend Moonglum, but his friend Moonglum does not remember me ..."

The remark seemed inconsequential to Corum.

"What does it mean to us, Jhary?"

"I do not know. Look — something else comes upon the stage."

There was a city upon a plain. Corum felt that he knew it, but then realised that he had never seen it before, for it was not like any city in Bro-an-Vadhagh or Lywm-an-Esh. Of white marble and black granite, it was simple and it was magnificent. It was under siege. Silver-snouted weapons were upon its walls, directed at the attackers — a great horde of cavalry and infantry which had pitched its tents below. The attackers were clad in massive armour, but the defenders wore light protection and they, too, like the one Jhary had called Elric, were more like the Vadhagh than like other mortals. Corum began to wonder if the Vadhagh occupied many planes.

A horseman in bulky armour rode from the camp towards the black and white walls of the city. He carried a banner and seemed to have come to parley. He called up at the walls and eventually a gate opened to admit him. The watchers could not see his face.

The scene changed again.

Now, strangely, the one who had been attacking the city was defending it.

Sudden glimpses of terrible massacres. The humans were being destroyed by weapons even more powerful than those possessed by the folk of Gwlãs-cor-Gwrys and it was one of their own kind who directed their murder ...

It was gone. Golden, pure light returned.

"Erekosë," murmured Jhary. "I think I see significance in these scenes. I think it is the Balance and it is hinting at something. But the implications are so profound that my poor head cannot contain them."

"Speak of them, please!" Corum begged into the darkness, his eyes still upon the golden stage.

"There are no words. I have told you already that I am a Companion to Champions —— that there is only one Champion and only one Companion, but that we do not always know each other, or even know of our fate.

Circumstances change from time to time, but the basic destiny does not. It was Erekosë's burden that he would be aware of this —— aware of all his previous incarnations, his incarnations to come. You, at least, are spared that, Corum."

Corum shuddered. "Say no more."

Rhalina said: "And what of this hero's lovers? You have spoken of his friend ..."

And a new scene came upon the golden stage before she could continue.

The face of a man, racked with pain, covered in sweat, a dark, throbbing jewel embedded in his forehead. He drew down over this face a helm of such highly polished metal that it became a perfect mirror. In the mirror could be seen a group of riders who at first appeared to be men with the heads of beasts. Then it became plain that those heads were in fact helmets fashioned to resemble pigs, goats, bulls and dogs.

There was a pitched battle. There were several riders in the same polished helms. They were greatly outnumbered by their enemies in the beasts-masks.

One of those in the mirror helmets —— perhaps the man they had first seen — held something aloft —— a short staff from which pulsed many-coloured rays. This staff struck fear into the beast riders and many had to be driven on by their leaders.

The fight continued.

The scene vanished to be replaced, once more, by nothing but the pure, golden light.

"Hawkmoon," murmured Jhary. "The Runestaff. What can all this mean? You have witnessed yourself, Corum, in three other incarnations. I have never experienced such a thing before."

Corum was trembling. He could not bear to consider Jhary's words. They suggested that it was his fate to experience an eternity of battle, of death, of misery.

"What can it mean?" Jhary said again. "Is it a warning? A

54

prediction of something about to take place? Or has it no special significance?"

Slowly the blackness descended on the golden light until there was only a faint line of gold and then that too, vanished.

They hung once more in limbo.

Jhary's voice came to Corum. The tone was distant as if the dandy spoke to himself. "I think it means we must find Tanelorn. There, all destinies meet — there, all things are constant. Neither Law nor Chaos can affect Tanelorn's existence, though her occupants can sometimes be threatened. But even I do not know where Tanelorn lies in this age, in these dimensions. If I could only discover some sign which would give me my bearings ..."

"Perhaps it is not Tanelorn we should seek," Rhalina said, "perhaps these events we have been shown indicate some different quest?"

"It is all bound up together," Jhary mused, seeming to answer a question he had put to himself. "It is all bound up together. Elric, Erekosë, Hawkmoon, Corum. Four aspects of the same thing, as I am another aspect of it, as Rhalina is a sixth aspect. Some disruption has occurred in the universe, perhaps. Or some new cycle as about to take place. I do not know ..."

The Sky Ship lurched. It moved as if along a crazily undulating track. Massive teardrops of green and blue light began to fall all around them. There was the sound of a raging wind, but no wind touched them. An almost human voice, echoing on and on and on.

And then they were flying through swiftly moving shadows — the shadows of things and people all rushing in the same direction.

Below Corum saw a thousand volcanoes, each one spewing red cinders and smoke, but somehow the cinders and smoke did not touch the Sky Ship. There was a stink of burning and it was suddenly replaced by the smell of flowers. The volcanoes had become so many huge blossoms, like anemones opening red petals.

Singing came from somewhere. A joyful, martial tune like the song of a victorious army. It died away. There was a laugh, cut off short.

The bulk of enormous beasts rose from seas of excrement

and the beasts raised their square snouts to the skies and groaned before sinking again beneath the surface.

A mottled, pink-white plain, apparently of stones. It was not stones. The plain was comprised entirely of corpses, each one neatly laid beside the other, each one face down.

"Where are we Jhary, do you know?" Corum called, peering through disturbed air at his friend.

"This place is ruled by Chaos, that is all I know at present, Corum. What you see is Chaos unbounded. Law has no power here at all. I believe we must be in Mabelode's Realm and I am attempting to take the Sky Ship out of it, but it will not respond."

"We are moving through the dimensions, however," Rhalina said. "The scenes change so rapidly. That must be the case."

Jhary offered her a desperate grin as he turned to look at her over his shoulder. "We are not moving through the dimensions. This is Chaos, Lady Rhalina. Pure, unchained Chaos."

The Second Chapter

THE CASTLE BUILT OF BLOOD

"It is surely Mabelode's Realm," Jhary said, "unless Chaos has conquered suddenly and all Fifteen Planes are once again under its domination."

Foul shapes flew about the Sky Ship for a moment and then were gone.

"My brain reels," Rhalina gasped. "It as if I am mad. I can hardly believe I do not dream."

"Someone dreams," Jhary told her. "Someone dreams, lady. A god."

Corum could not speak. His head was aching. Peculiar memories threatened to come to him, but they remained elusive.

Sometimes he would listen hard, believing that he heard voices. He would peer over the rail of the craft to see if they came from beneath the ship. He would stare into the sky. "Do you hear them, Rhalina?"

"I hear nothing, Corum."

"I cannot make out the words. Perhaps they are not words."

"Forget them," Jhary said sharply. "Pay no attention to anything of that sort. We are in Chaos lands and our senses will deceive us in every way. Remember that we three are the only realities —— and be careful to inspect anything which looks like me or Rhalina very carefully before you trust it."

"You mean demons will try to make me think that they are those I love?"

"That is what they will do, call them what you will."

A huge wave advanced towards them. It took the form of a human hand. It clenched itself into a fist. It threatened to smash the boat. It disappeared. Jhary flew on. He was sweating.

A spring day dawned. They flew over the morning fields as the dew sparkled. Flowers grew in the dew and there were little bright pools of water, tiny rivers. In the shade of oak-trees stood horses and cows. A little way ahead was a low, white farmhouse with smoke curling from its chimney. Birds sang. Pigs rooted in the farmyard.

"I cannot believe it is not real," Corum said to Jhary.

"It is real," Jhary told him. "But it is short-lived. Chaos delights in creation but swiftly becomes bored with what it creates for it seeks not order or justice or constancy but sensation, entertainment. Sometimes it suits it to create something which you and I would value or find pleasure in. But it is an accident."

The fields remained. The farmhouse remained. The sense of peace grew.

Jhary frowned. "Perhaps, after all, we have left the Realm of Chaos and …"

The fields gradually began to swirl, like stagnant water stirred by a stick. The farmhouse spread to become scum on top of the water. The flowers were now festering growths on the surface.

"It becomes so easy to believe what one wishes to believe," Jhary said wearily. "So easy."

"We must escape from here," said Corum.

"Escape? I cannot control the Sky Ship. I have not controlled it since we entered limbo."

"Then some other force controls us?"

"Aye —— but it may not be sentient." Jhary's voice was strained, his face was pale. Even the little cat was nestling hard against his neck as if seeking comfort.

Stretching to every horizon now was seething stuff, greyish-green with what looked like pieces of rotting vegetation floating in it. The vegetation seemed to assume the shapes of crustaceans —— crabs and lobsters scuttling across its surface, only slightly different in shade.

"An island," Rhalina said.

Out of all this rose an island of dark blue rock. Upon the rock was a building, a great castle all coloured scarlet. And the scarlet rippled as if water had somehow been moulded into a permanent shape. A familiar, salty smell came from the scarlet castle. Jhary turned the ship to avoid it, but then the castle was ahead of them again. Again he turned. Again it was ahead of them. For several moments he altered the course of the Sky Ship and each time the castle reappeared before them.

"It seeks to stop us." Jhary tried again to avoid it.

"What is it?" Rhalina asked.

Jhary shook his head. "I know not, but it is unlike the other things we have seen. We are being drawn towards it now. That stench! It clogs my nostrils!"

Closer came the Sky Ship until it hovered directly above the scarlet turrets of the castle. And then it had landed.

Corum peered over the side. The substance of the castle still rippled like liquid. It did not look solid, yet it held the Sky Ship. He drew his sword and looked towards a black gap in the near by tower. An entrance. And a figure was emerging from it.

The figure was fat, about twice as broad as an ordinary man. It had a head which was essentially human but from which boar-like tusks sprouted. It moved over the rippling scarlet surface on bowed, thick legs, naked but for a tabard embroidered with a design not immediately recognisable. It was grinning at them. "I have been short of guests," it grunted. "Are you mine?"

Corum said: "Your guests?"

"No, no, no. Did I make you or did you come from elsewhere. Are you inventions of one of my brother dukes?"

"I do not understand —— " Corum began.

Jhary interrupted him. "I know you. You are Duke Teer."

"Of course I am Duke Teer. What of it? Why, I do not believe you are inventions at all — not of this Realm at all. How satisfying. Welcome, mortals, to my castle. How remarkable! Welcome, welcome, welcome. How exquisite! Welcome!"

"You are Duke Teer of Chaos and your liege lord is Mabelode the Faceless. I was right, then. This is King Mabelode's Realm."

"How intelligent! How marvellous!" The boar face split in an ugly grin and rotting teeth were displayed. "Do you bring me some message, perhaps?"

"We, too, serve King Mabelode," Jhary said swiftly. "We fight in Arkyn's Realm to restore the rule of Chaos there."

"How excellent! But do not say you come for aid, mortals, for all my aid already goes to that other Realm where Law attempts to hold sway. Every Duke of Hell sends his resources to the fight. The time might yet arise when we can go personally to do battle with Law, but that is not yet. We lend our powers, our servants, everything but ourselves — for doubtless you have learned what became of Xiombarg when he — or she, I should say, of course — attempted to cross into Arkyn's Realm. How unpleasant!"

"We had hoped for aid," Corum said, falling in with Jhary's attempted deception. "Law has thwarted us too often."

"I, as you know, am only a minor Lord of Chaos. My powers have never been great. Most of my efforts have gone — and peers may laugh — into the creation of my beautiful castle. I love it so much."

"What is it made of?" Rhalina asked him nervously. She plainly did not think they could remain undetected for long.

"You have not heard of Teer's castle? How strange! Why, my pretty mortal, it is built of blood — it is built all of blood. Many thousands have died to make my castle. I must slay many thousands more before it is properly completed. Blood, my dear — blood and blood and blood! Can you not sniff its delicious tang? What you sniff is blood. What you see — it is all blood. Mortal blood — immortal blood — it all mingles. All blood is equal when it goes to build Teer's castle, eh? Why, you have blood enough for part of a small wall of a tower. I could make a room from all three of you. You would be astonished to learn how far blood can be made to stretch as a building material. And it is tasty, eh?" He shrugged and waved a thick hand. "Or perhaps not to you. I know mortals and their fads. But for me —— ah, it is delightful!"

"It was an honour to see the famous Castle Built of Blood," Jhary said as smoothly as he could, "but now the business of the moment presses and we must go to seek help in our fight against Law. Will you allow us to leave now, Duke Teer?"

"Leave?" The small eyes glinted. A fat, rough tongue licked the coarse lips. Teer fingered one of his tusks.

"We are, after all, upon King Mabelode's service," said Corum.

"So you are! How superb!"

"It is urgent, our quest."

"It is rare for mortals to come directly to King Mabelode's Realm," Duke Teer said.

"These are rare times, with two of our Realms in the hands of Law," Jhary pointed out.

"How true! What is that running from the lips of the female?"

Rhalina was vomiting. She had done all she could to contain her nausea, but the stink had become too much for her.

Duke Teer's eyes narrowed. "I know mortals. I know them. She is distressed. By what? By what?"

"By the thought of Law's return," said Jhary weakly.

"She is distressed by me, eh? She is not wholly given up to serving Chaos, eh? Not a very good specimen for King Mabelode to pick to serve him, eh?"

"He picked us," Corum said. "She merely accompanies us."

"Then she is of little use to King Mabelode —— or to you. Here, then, is what I want in return for my allowing you to see the splendour of my Castle Built of Blood ..."

"No," said Corum, guessing what he meant. "We cannot do that. Let us go now, I beg you, Duke Teer. You know we must make haste! King Mabelode will not be pleased if you delay us."

"He will not be pleased with you if you delay. Simply give me the female. Keep the flesh and bones, if you desire. All I require is the blood."

"No!" screamed Rhalina in terror.

"How stupid!"

"Let us go, Duke Teer!"

"Let me have the female first!"

"No!" said Jhary and Corum in unison. And they drew their swords, whereupon Duke Teer burst into grunting laughter that was at once mocking and incredulous.

The Third Chapter

THE RIDER ON THE YELLOW HORSE

The Duke of Hell stretched as a man might stretch when awakening from a luxurious sleep. His arms grew longer, his body wider and, within a space of seconds, he had doubled his size. He looked down on them, still laughing. "How badly you lie!"

"We do not lie!" cried Corum. "We beg you —— let us be on our way."

Duke Teer frowned. "I have no wish to earn King Mabelode's displeasure. Yet if you truly served Chaos you would not show such silly emotions —— you would give the female to me. She is useless to you, but she can be of great use to me. I exist only to build my castle, make it more elaborate, more beautiful." He began to stretch out one great hand. "Here, I will take her and then you may go your way and I'll ——"

"See," called Jhary suddenly. "Our enemies! They have followed us to this plain. How stupid of them —— to cross into the Realm of their enemy King Mabelode."

"What?" Duke Teer looked up. He saw the score of black flying things with their long necks and their red jaws, the men upon their backs. "Who are they?"

"Their leader is called Corum Jhaelen Irsei," said Corum. "They are sworn enemies of Chaos and desire our deaths. Destroy them, Duke Teer, and Mabelode will be mightily pleased with you."

Duke Teer glared upwards. "Is this truth?"

"It is!" Jhary shouted.

"I believe I have heard of this mortal, Corum. Was it not

61

he who destroyed Arioch's heart? Is he the one who lured Xiombarg to her doom?"

"He is the same!" Rhalina cried.

"My nets," muttered Duke Teer, reducing his size and hurrying back into his tower. "I will help you."

"There is enough blood in them to build a whole new hall!" Jhary yelled. He leapt for the controls and hastily passed his hands over them. They came to life and the Sky Ship sprang into the air.

Glandyth and his flying pack had seen them. The black beasts turned, wings sounding like thunder, and sped towards the Sky Ship.

But they were free of the Castle Built of Blood now and Duke Teer was engaged with his nets. He had one in each hand and he grew larger and larger, casting towards the disconcerted Earl of Krae.

Jhary's face was set. "I am going to try everything I can to hurl the Sky Ship from this foul dimension," he said. "It will be better to die than remain here. Duke Teer will learn soon enough that Glandyth serves Chaos and not Law. And Glandyth will tell him who we are. All the Dukes of Hell will seek us out." He removed a transparent cover and began to rearrange the crystals. "I know not what this will accomplish, but I am determined to try to find out!"

The Sky Ship began to oscillate throughout its length. Clinging to the rail Corum felt his entire body vibrate until he was sure he would shake to pieces. He clung to Rhalina. The ship began to dive towards a sea of violet and orange. They were flung forward, upon Jhary. The ship struck something. They passed into a liquid which stifled them. Another mighty wrench and Corum lost his grasp on Rhalina. Through the darkness he tried to find her, but she had gone. He felt his feet leave the deck of the ship.

He began to drift.

He tried to call her name, but the stuff blocked his mouth. He tried to peer through it, but it stuck to his eyes.

He drifted languidly, sinking deeper and deeper. His heart began to bang against his chest. No air entered his lungs. He know he was dying.

And he knew Rhalina and Jhary were dying, somewhere nearby in the viscous stuff.

He was almost relieved that his quest had ended so, that his responsibility to the Cause of Law was over. He grieved for

Rhalina and he grieved for Jhary, but he could not grieve for himself.

Suddenly he was falling. He saw a piece of the Sky Ship —— a twisted rail —— fall with him. He was falling through clear air but the speed of his descent still made it impossible for him to breathe.

He began to glide. He looked about him. There was blue sky on all sides —— below him, above him. He spread his arms. The piece of twisted rail was still gliding with him. He looked for Rhalina. He looked for Jhary. They were nowhere in sight in all the blue vastness. There was just the piece of rail.

He called out:

"Rhalina?"

There was no reply.

He was alone in a universe of blue light.

He began to feel drowsy. His eyes closed. He fought to open them but he could not. It was as if his brain refused any longer to experience further terrors.

When he awoke he was lying on something soft and very comfortable. He felt warm and he realised he was naked. He opened his eyes and saw the beams of a roof above him. He turned his head. He was in a room. Sunlight came through a window.

Was this a further illusion? The room was plainly at the top of a house, for its walls sloped. It was simply furnished. The home of a well-to-do peasant farmer, Corum thought. He looked at the varnished door with its simple metal latch. He heard a voice singing behind it.

How had he come here? It was possible that it was a trick. Jhary had warned him to beware of such visions. He drew his hands from beneath the bedsheets. On his left wrist there still remained the Hand of Kwll, six-fingered and bejewelled. He touched his face. The Eye of Rhynn, useless though it now was, still filled the socket of his right eye. On a chest in one corner all his clothes had been laid and his weapons were stacked near by.

Had he somehow returned to his own plane and had sanity been restored to it. Could Duke Teer have slain Glandyth and thus lifted Glandyth's spell from the land?

The room was not familiar, neither were the designs on the

chest and the bed-posts. This was not, he was sure, Lywm-an-Esh and it was most certainly not Bro-an-Vadhagh.

The door opened and a fat man entered. He looked amused and said something which Corum could not understand.

"Do you speak the language of Vadhagh or Mabden?" Corum asked him politely.

The fat man — not a farmer by his embroidered shirt and silk breeks — shook his head and spread his hands, speaking again in the strange language.

"Where is this place?" Corum asked him.

The fat man pointed out of the window, pointed to the floor, spoke at some length, laughed and indicated with further gestures that Corum might like to eat. Corum nodded. He was very hungry.

Before the man left, he said: "Rhalina? Jhary?" hoping that he would recognise the names and know where the two were. The man shook his head, laughed again and closed the door behind him.

Corum got up. He felt weak but not totally weary. He pulled on his clothes, picked up the byrnie and then laid it down again with the helm and the greaves. He went to the door and peered out. He saw a landing, varnished with the same brown varnish, a staircase leading downward. He stepped onto the landing and tried to peer below, but saw only another landing. He heard voices — a woman's voice, the laughter of the fat man. He went back into the room and looked out of the window.

The house lay on the outskirts of a town. But it was not a town like any he had seen before. All the houses had red, sloping roofs and were built of a mixture of timber and grey brick. The streets were cobbled and carts passed this way and that along them. Most of the people wore drabber clothes than those he had seen on the fat man, but they looked cheerful enough, often calling out greetings to each other, stopping to pass the time of day.

The town seemed quite large and in the distance Corum could see a wall, the spires of taller buildings plainly more expensively built than the ordinary houses. Sometimes carriages passed by, or well-dressed men on horseback made their way through the throng — nobles or possibly merchants.

Corum rubbed his head and went to sit on the edge of the bed. He tried to think clearly. The evidence was that he was on another plane. And there seemed to be no battle between

Law and Chaos here. Everyone was, as far as he could tell, leading ordinary, sedate lives. Yet he had it both from Lord Arkyn and from Duke Teer that every one of the Fifteen Planes was in conflict as Law fought Chaos. Was this some plane ruled by Arkyn or his brother which had not yet succumbed? It was unlikely. And he could not speak the language while they could not understand him. That had never happened to him before. Jhary's rearrangement of the crystals before the Sky Ship had been destroyed had evidently produced a drastic result. He was cut off from anything he knew. He might never learn where he was. And all this suggested that Rhalina and Jhary, if they lived, were similarly abandoned on some unfamiliar plane.

The fat man opened the door and an equally fat woman in voluminous white skirts entered the room with a tray on which was arranged meat, vegetables, fruit and a steaming bowl of soup. She smiled at him and offered him the tray rather as if she were offering food to a caged wild animal. He bowed and smiled and took the tray. She was careful to avoid touching his six-fingered hand.

"You are kind," said Corum, knowing she would not understand. but wishing her to know that he was grateful. While they watched, he began to eat. The food was not particularly well-cooked or flavoured, but he was hungry. He ate it all as gracefully as he could and eventually with another bow, returned the tray to the silent pair.

He had eaten too much too swiftly and his stomach felt heavy. He had never been much attracted to Mabden food at any time and this was coarser than most. But he made a great pretence of being satisfied, for he had become unused to kindness of late.

Now the fat man asked another question. It sounded like a single word. "Fenk?"

"Fenk?" said Corum and shook his head.

"Fenk?"

Again Corum shook his head.

"Pannis?"

Another shake of the head. There were several more questions of the same sort — just a single word — and each time Corum indicated that he did not understand. Now it was his turn. He tried several words in the Mabden dialect, a language derived from Vadhagh. The man did not understand. He pointed at Corum's six-fingered hand, frowning, pulling

65

at one of his own hands, chopping at it, until Corum realised that he was asking if the hand had been lost in battle and this was an artificial one. Corum nodded rapidly and smiled, tapping at his eye also. The man seemed satisfied but extremely curious. He inspected the hand, marvelling. Doubtless he believed it to be mortal work and Corum could not explain that it had been grafted to him by means of sorcery. The man indicated that Corum should come with him through the door. Corum willingly consented and was led down the stairs and into what was plainly a workshop.

And now he understood. The man was a maker of artificial limbs. He was plainly experimenting with many different kinds. There were wooden, bone and metal legs, some of them of very complicated manufacture. There were hands carved from ivory or made of jointed steel. There were arms, feet, even something which seemed to be a steel rib-cage. There were also many anatomical drawings in a peculiar, alien style and Corum was fascinated by them. He saw a pile of scrolls bound into single sheets between leather covers and he opened one. It seemed to be a book concerning medicine. Although cruder in design and although the strange, angular letters were not at all beautiful in themselves, the book seemed as sophisticated as many which the Vadhagh had created before the coming of the Mabden. He tapped the book and made an approving noise.

"It is good," he said.

The man smiled and tapped again at Corum's hand. Corum wondered what the doctor would say if he could explain how he came by it. The poor man would probably be horrified or, perhaps more likely, convinced that Corum was mad, as Corum would have been before he began to encounter sorcery.

Corum let the doctor inspect the eye-patch and the peculiar eye beneath it.

This puzzled the fat man even more. He shook his head, frowning. Corum lowered the patch back over the eye. He half-wished that he could demonstrate to the doctor exactly what the eye and the hand were used for.

Corum began to guess how he had come here. Evidently some citizens had found him unconscious and sent for the doctor, or brought Corum to the doctor. The doctor, obsessed with his study of artificial limbs, had been only too pleased to

66

take Corum in, though what he had made of Corum's arms and armour the Prince in the Scarlet Robe did not know.

But now Corum became filled with a sense of urgency, with fears for Rhalina and Jhary. If they were in this world he must find them. It was even possible that Jhary, who had travelled so often between the planes, could speak the language. He took up a piece of blank parchment and a quill, dipped the quill in ink (it was little different to the pens used by the Mabden) and drew a picture of a man and a woman. He held up two fingers and pointed outside, frowning and gesturing to show that he did not know where they were. The fat doctor nodded vigorously, understanding. But then he showed, almost comically, that he did not know where Jhary and Rhalina were, that he had not seen them, that Corum had been found alone.

"I must look for them," Corum said urgently, pointing to himself and then ponting out of the house. The doctor understood and nodded. He thought for a moment and then signed for Corum to stay there. He left and returned wearing a jerkin. He gave Corum a plain cloak to wrap around his clothes which were, for the place, outlandish. Together they left the house.

Many glanced at Corum as he and the doctor walked through the streets. Obviously the news of the stranger had gone everywhere. The doctor led Corum through the crowds and beneath an arch through the wall. A white, dusty road led through fields. There were one or two farmhouses in the distance.

They came eventually to a small wood and here the doctor stopped, showing Corum where he had been found. Corum looked about him and at last discovered the thing he sought. It was the twisted rail of the Sky Ship. He showed it to the doctor who had certainly seen nothing like it, for he gasped in astonishment, turning it this way and that in his hands.

It was proof to Corum that he had not gone mad, that he had but recently left the Realm of Chaos.

He looked around him at the peaceful scenery. Were there really such places where the eternal struggle was unknown? He began to feel jealous of the inhabitants of this plane. Doubtless they had their own sorrows and discomforts. Evidently there was war and pain, for why else would the doctor be so interested in making artifical limbs? And yet there was a sense of order here and he was sure that no gods —— either of Law or Chaos —— existed here. But he knew that it would be stupid to entertain the idea of remaining here, for he was not like them, he hardly resembled them physically, even. He wondered what speculations the doctor had made to explain his coming here.

He began to walk amongst the trees, calling out the names of Rhalina and Jhary.

He heard a cry later and whirled round, hoping it was the woman he loved. But it was not. It was a tall, grim-faced man in a black gown, striding across the fields towards them, his grey hair blowing in the breeze. The doctor approached him and they began to converse, looking often at Corum who stood watching them. There was a dispute between them and both became angrier. The newcomer pointed a long, accusing finger at Corum and waved his other hand.

Corum felt trepidation, wishing he had brought his sword with him.

Suddenly the man in the robe turned and marched back towards the town, leaving the doctor frowning and rubbing at his jowl.

Corum became nervous, sensing that something was wrong, that the man in the robe objected to his presence in the town, was suspicious of his peculiar physical appearance. And the man in the robe also seemed to have more authority than the doctor. And far less sympathy for Corum.

Head bowed, the doctor moved towards Corum. He raised his head, his lips pursed. He murmured something in his own language, speaking to Corum as a man might speak to a pet for which he had great affection —— a pet which was about to be killed or sent away.

Corum decided that he must have his armour and weapons at once. He pointed towards the town and began to walk back. The doctor followed, still deep in worried thought.

Back in the doctor's house Corum donned his silver byrnie, his silver greaves and silver helm. He buckled on his long strong sword and looped his bow, his arrows and his lance upon his back. He realised that he looked more incongruous than ever, but he also felt more secure. He looked out of the window at the street. Night was falling. Only a few people walked in the town now. He left the room and went down the stairs to the main door of the house. The doctor shouted at him and tried to stop him from leaving, but Corum gently brushed him aside, opened the latch and went out.

The doctor called to him —— a warning cry. But Corum ignored it, both because he did not need to be warned of potential danger and also because he did not see why the kindly man should share his danger. He strode into the night.

Few saw him. None stopped him or even tried to do so, though they peered curiously at him and laughed among themselves, evidently taking him for an idiot. It was better that they laughed at him than feared him, or else the danger would have been much increased, thought Corum.

He strode through the street for some time until he came to a partially ruined house which had been deserted. He decided that he would make this his resting place for the night, hiding here until he could think of his next action.

He stumbled through the broken door and rats fled as he entered. He climbed the swaying staircase until he came to a room with a window through which he could observe the street. He was hardly aware of his own reasons for leaving the doctor's house, save that he did not wish to become involved with the man in the robe. If they were seriously trying to find him, then, of course, they would discover him soon enough. But if they had a little superstition, they might think he had vanished as mysteriously as he had arrived.

He settled down to sleep, ignoring the sound the rats made.

He woke at dawn and peered down into the street. This seemed to be the main street of the city and it was already alive with tradesmen and others, some with donkeys or horses, others with handcarts, calling out greetings to each other.

He smelled fresh bread and began to feel hungry, but curbed his impulse, when a baker's cart stopped immediately beneath him, to sneak out and steal a loaf. He dozed again. When it was night, he would try to find a horse and leave the city behind him, seek other towns where there might be news of Rhalina or Jhary.

Towards midday he heard a great deal of cheering in the street and he edged his way to the window.

There were flags waving and a band of some sort was playing raucous music. A procession was marching through the streets — a martial procession by the look of it, for many of the riders were undoubtebly warriors in their steel breast-plates and with their swords and lances.

In the middle of the procession, hardly acknowledging the crowd's cheers, was the man who was the object of their cele-bration. He rode a big yellow horse and he wore a high-collared red cloak which at first hid his face from Co-rum. There was a hat on his head, a sword at his side. He was frowning a little.

Then Corum saw with mild surprise that the man's left hand was missing. He clutched his reins in a specially made hook device. The warrior turned his head and Corum was this time completely astonished. He gasped, for the man on the yellow horse had an eye-patch over his right eye. And, though his face was of the Mabden cast, he bore a strong resemblance to Corum.

Corum stood up, about to cry out to the man who was al-most his double. But then he felt a hand close over his mouth and strong arms bear him down to the floor.

He wrenched his head about to see who attacked him. His eyes widened.

"Jhary!" he said. "So you are on this plane! And Rhalina? Have you seen her?"

The dandy, who was dressed in the clothes of the local in-habitants, shook his head. "I have not. I had hoped that you and she stayed together. You have made yourself conspicuous here, I gather."

"Do you know this plane?"

"I know it vaguely. I can speak one or two of their lan-guages."

"And the man on the yellow horse — who is he?"

"He is the reason why you should leave here as soon as pos-sible. He is yourself, Corum. He is your incarnation on this plane in this age. And it goes against all the laws of the cos-mos that you and he should occupy the same plane at the same time. We are in great danger, Corum, but these folk could also be in danger if we continue — however unwittingly — to disrupt the order, the very balance of the multiverse."

The Fourth Chapter

THE MANOR IN THE FOREST

"You know this world, Jhary?"

The dandy put a finger to his lips and drew Corum into the shadows as the parade went by. "I know most worlds," he murmured, "but this less well than many. The Sky Ship's destruction flung us through time as well as through the dimensions and we are marooned in a world whose logic is in most cases essentially different. Secondly our 'selves' exist here and we therefore threaten to upset the fine balance of this age and, doubtless, others, too. To create paradoxes in a world not used to them would be dangerous, you see ..."

"Then let us leave this world with all speed! Let us find Rhalina and go!"

Jhary smiled. "We cannot leave an age and a plane as we would leave a room, as you well know. Besides, I do not believe Rhalina to be here if she has not been seen. But that can be discovered. There used to be a lady not far from here who was something of a seeress. I am hoping that she will help us. The folk of this age have an uncommon respect for people like ourselves — though often that respect turns to hatred and they hound us. You know you are sought by a priest who wants to burn you at the stake?"

"I know a man disliked me".

Jhary laughed. "Aye — disliked you enough to want to torture you to death. He is a dignitary of their religion. He has great power and has already called out warriors to search for you. We must get horses as soon as possible."

Jhary paced the rickety floor, stroking his chin. "We must return to the Fifteen Planes with all speed. We have no right to be here ..."

"And no wish to be," Corum reminded him.

Outside the sound of pipes and drums faded and the crowd began to disperse.

"I remember her name now!" Jhary muttered. He snapped

his fingers. "It is the Lady Jane Pentallyon and she dwells in a house close to a village called Warleggon."

"These are strange names, Jhary-a-Conel!"

"No stranger than ours are to them. We must make speed for Warleggon as soon as possible and we must pray that Lady Jane Rentallyon is in residence and has not, herself, been burned by now."

Corum stepped closer to the window and glanced down. "The priest comes," he said, "with his men."

"I thought it likely you would be seen entering here. They have waited until after the parade lest you escaped in the confusion. I like not the thought of killing them, when we have no business in their age at all ..."

"And I like not the thought of being killed," Corum pointed out. He drew his long, strong sword and made for the stairs.

He was half-way down when the first of them burst in, the priest in the gown at their head. He called out to them and made a sign at Corum — doubtless some superstitious Mabden charm. Corum sprang forward and stabbed him in the throat, his single eye blazing fiercely. The warriors gasped at this. Evidently they had not expected their leader to die so soon. They hesitated in the doorway

Jhary said softly from behind Corum: "That was foolish. They take it ill when their holy men are slain. Now the whole town will be against us and our leavetaking will be the harder."

Corum shrugged and began to advance towards the three warriors crowded in the doorway. "These men have horses. Let us take them and have done with it, Jhary. I am weary of hesitation. Defend yourselves, Mabden!"

The Mabden parried his thrusts but, in so doing, became entangled with each other. Corum took one in the heart and wounded another in the hand. The pair fled into the street yelling.

Corum and Jhary followed, though Jhary's face was set and disapproving. He preferred subtler plans than this. But his own sword whisked out to take the life of a mounted man who tried to ride him down and he pushed the body from the saddle, leaping upon the back of the horse. It reared and arched its neck but Jhary got it under control and defended himself against two more riders who came at him from the end of the street.

Corum was still on his feet. He used his jewelled hand as a club, forcing his way through to where several horses stood without riders. The Mabden were terrified, it seemed, of the touch of his six-fingered, alien hand and dodged to avoid it. Two more died before Corum reached the horses and sprang into the saddle. He called out:

"Which way, Jhary?"

"This way!" Without looking behind him, Jhary galloped the horse down the street.

Striking aside one who tried to grab at his reins Corum followed the dandy. A great hubbub began to spread through the city as they raced towards the west wall. Tradesmen and peasants tried to block their path, they were forced to leap over carts and force a path through cattle or sheep. More warriors were coming, too, from two sides.

And then they had ducked under the archway and were through the low wall and riding swiftly down the white, dusty road away from the city, a pack of warriors at their backs.

Arrows began to whistle past their heads as archers came to the walls and shot at them Corum was astonished at the range of the bowmen. "Are these sorcerous arrows, Jhary?"

"No! It is a kind of bow unknown in your age. These people are masters of it. We are lucky, however, that it is too bulky a bow to be shot from a horse. There, see, the arrows are beginning to fall short. But the horsemen stay with us. Into yonder wood, Corum. Swiftly!"

They plunged off the road and into a deep, sweet-smelling forest, leaping a small stream, the horses' hoofs slipping for a moment in damp moss.

"How will the doctor fare?" Corum called. "The one who took me in."

"He will die unless he is clever and denounces you," Jhary told him.

"But he was a man of great intelligence and humanity. A man of science, too — of learning."

"All the more reason for killing him, if their priesthood has its way. Superstition, not learning, is respected here."

"Yet it is such a pleasant land. The people seem well-meaning and kind!"

"You can say that, with those warriors at our backs?" Jhary laughed as he slapped his horse's rump to make it gallop faster. "You have seen too much of Glandyth and his kind, of Chaos and the like, if this seems paradise to you!"

"Compared with what we have left behind, it is paradise, Jhary."

"Aye, perhaps you speak truth."

By much back-tracking and hiding they had managed to throw off their pursuers before sunset and they now walked along a narrow track, leading their tired horses.

"It is a good many miles to Warleggon yet," Jhary said. "I would thatI had a map, Prince Corum, to guide us, for it was in another body with different eyes that I last saw this land."

"What is the land itself called?" asked the Prince in the Scarlet Robe.

"It is, like Lym-an-Esh, divided into a number of lands under the dominion of one monarch. This one is called Kernow — or Cornwall, depending whether you speak the language of the region or the language of the realm as a whole. It's a superstition-ridden land, though its traditions go back further than most other parts of the country of which it is part, and you will find much of it like your own Bro-an-Vadhagh. Its memories stretch back longer than do the memories of the rest of the realm. The memories have darkened, but they still have partial legends of a people like yourself who once lived here."

"You mean this Kernow lies in my future?"

"In one future, probably not yours. The future of a corresponding plane, perhaps. There are doubtless other futures where the Vadhagh have proliferated and the Mabden died out. The multiverse contains, after all, an infinity of possibilities."

"Your knowledge is great, Jhary-a-Conel."

The dandy reached into his shirt and drew out his little black and white cat. It had been there all the time they had been fighting and escaping. It began to purr, stretching its limbs and its wings. It settled on Jhary's shoulder.

"My knowledge is partial," said Jhary wearily. "It consists generally of half-memories."

"But why do you know so much of this plane?"

"Because I dwell here even now. There is really no such thing as time, you see. I remember what to you is the 'future'. I remember one of my many incarnations. If you had watched the parade longer you would have seen not only yourself but myself. I am called by some grand title here, but I serve the one you saw on the yellow horse. He was born in

74

that city we have left and he is reckoned a great soldier by these people, though, like you, I think he would prefer peace to war. That is the fate of the Champion Eternal."

"I'll hear no more of that," Corum said quickly. "It disturbs me too much."

"I cannot blame you."

They stopped at last to water their horses and take turns to sleep. Sometimes in the distance groups of horsemen would ride by, their brands flaring in the night, but they never came close enough to be a great threat.

In the morning they reached the edges of a wide expanse of heather. A light rain fell but it did not discomfort them, rather it refreshed them. Their sure-footed horses began to canter over the moor and brought them soon to a valley and a forest.

"We have skirted Warleggon now," said Jhary. "I thought it wise. But there is the forest I sought. See the smoke rising deep within. That, I hope, is the manor of the Lady Jane."

Along a winding path protected on each side by high banks of rich-scented moss and wild flowers they rode and there at last were two posts of brown stone which were topped by two carvings of spread-winged hawks, mellowed by the weather. The gates of bent iron were open and they walked their horses along a gravel path until they turned a corner and saw the house. It was a large house of three storeys, made of the same light brown stone, with a grey slate roof and five chimneys of a reddish tint. Lattice windows were set into the house and there was a low doorway in the centre.

Two old men came round the side of the house at the sound of their horses' hoofs on the gravel. The men had dark features, heavy brows, long, grey hair. They were dressed in leather and skins and, if they wore any expression at all, their eyes seemed to hold a look of grim satisfaction as they looked at Corum in his high helm and his silver byrnie.

Jhary spoke to them in their own language — a language which was not that Corum had heard in the city but a language which seemed to hold faint echoes of the Vadhagh speech.

One of the men took their horses to be stabled. The other entered the house by the main door. Corum and Jhary waited without.

And then she came to the door.

She was an old, beautiful woman, her long hair pure white

75

and braided, a mantle upon her brow. She wore a flowing gown of light blue silk, with wide sleeves and gold embroidery at neck and hem.

Jhary spoke to her in her own tongue, but she smiled then.

She spoke in the pure, rippling speech of the Vadhagh.

"I know who you are," she said. "We have been waiting for you here at the Manor in the Forest."

The Fifth Chapter

THE LADY JANE PENTALLYON

The old, beautiful lady led them into the cool room. Meats and wines and fruits were upon the table of polished oak. Jars of flowers everywhere made the air sweet. She looked at Corum more often than she looked at Jhary. And at Corum she looked almost fondly.

Corum removed his helm with a bow. "We thank you, lady, for this gracious hospitality. I find much kindness in your land, as well as hatred."

She smiled, nodding. "Some are kind," she said, "but not many. The elf folk as a race are kinder."

He said politely: "The elf folk, lady?"

"Your folk."

Jhary removed a crumpled hat from within his jerkin. It was the hat he always wore. He looked at it sorrowfully. "It will take much to straighten that to its proper shape. These adventures are hardest of all on hats, I fear. The Lady Jane Pentallyon speaks of the Vadhagh race, Prince Corum, or their kin, the Eldren, who are not greatly different, save for the eyes, just as the Melniboneans and the Nilanrians are off-shoots of the same race. In this land they are known some-times as Elves — sometimes as devils, djins, even gods, de-pending upon the region."

"I am sorry," said the Lady Jane Pentallyon gently. "I had

forgotton that your people prefers to use its own names for its race. And yet the name "Elf" is sweet to my years, just as it is sweet to speak your language again after so many years."

"Call me what you will, lady," Corum said gallantly, "for almost certainly I owe you my life and, perhaps, my peace of mind. How came you to learn our tongue?"

"Eat," she said. "I have made the food as tender as I could, knowing that the elf folk have more delicate palates than we. I will tell you my story while you banish your hunger."

And Corum began to eat, discovering that this was the finest Mabden food he had ever eaten. Compared with the food he had had in the town it was light as air and delicately flavoured. The Lady Jane Pentallyon began to speak, her voice distant and nostalgic.

"I was a girl," she said, "of seventeen years, and I was already mistress of this manor, for my father had died crusading and my mother had contracted the plague while on a visit to her sister. So, too, had my little brother died, for she had taken him with her. I was distressed, of course, but not old enough to know then that the best way of dealing with sorrow is to face it, not try to escape it. I affected not to care that all my family were dead. I took to reading romances and to dreaming of myself as a Guinevere or an Isolde. These servants you have seen were with me then and they seemed little younger in those days. They respected my moods and there was none to check me as a kind of quiet madness came over me and I dwelt more and more in my own dreams and less and less thought of the world which, anyway, was far away and sent no news. And then one day there came an Egyptian tribe past the manor and they begged permission to set up their camp in a glade in the woods not far from here. I had never seen such strange, dark faces and glittering black eyes and I was fascinated by them and believed them to be the guardians of magic wisdom such as Merlin had known. I know now that most of them knew nothing at all. But there was one girl of my own age who had been orphaned like me and with whom I identified myself. She was dark and I was fair, but we were of a height and shape and, doubtless because narcissium had become one of my faults, I invited her to live in the house with me after the rest of the tribe had moved on — taking, I need not say, much of our livestock with them.

77

But I did not care, for Aireda's tales — learned from her parents, I understood — were far wilder than any I had read in my books or imagined for myself. She spoke of dark old ones who could still be summoned to carry young girls off to lands of magic delight, to worlds where great demigods with magic swords disrupted the very stuff of nature if their moods willed it. I think now that Aireda was inventing much of what she told me — elaborating stories she had heard from her mother and father — but the essence of what she told me was, of course, true. Aireda had learned spells which, she said, would summon these beings, but she was afraid to use them. I begged her to conjure each of us a god from another world to be our lovers, but she became afraid and would not. A year passed and our deep, dark games went on, our minds became more and more full of the idea of magic and demons and gods and Aireda, at my constant behest, slowly weakened in her resolve not to speak the spells and perform the rituals she knew ..."

The Lady Jane Pentallyon took up a dish of sliced fruit and offered it to Corum. He accepted it. "Please continue, lady."

"Well, I learned from her the patterns to carve upon the stones of the floor, the herbs to brew, the arrangements of precious stones and particular kinds of rocks, of candles and the like. I got from her every piece of knowledge save the incantations and the signs which must be traced in the air with a witch-knife of glowing crystal. So I carved the patterns in the stones, I gathered the herbs, I collected the stones and the rocks and I sent to the city for the candles. And I presented them all to Aireda one day, telling her that she must call for the old ones who ruled this land before the Druids who, themselves, came before the Christians. And she agreed to do it, for by this time she had become as mad as me. We chose All-Hallows Eve for the ritual, though I do not believe now that it has any special significance. We arranged the stones and the rocks and we traced the designs in the air with the crystal witch-knife and we burned the candles and we brewed the herbs and we drank what we brewed and we were successful ..."

Jhary sat back in his chair, his eyes fixed on the Lady Jane Pentallyon. He was eating an apple. "You were successful, lady," he said, "in conjuring up a demon?"

"A demon? I think not, though he looked to us like a demon with his slanting eyes and his pointed ears — a face not unlike

78

your own, Prince Corum — and we were at first afraid for he stood in the centre of our magic ring and he was furious, shouting, threatening in a language which I could not, in those days, understand. Well, the tale grows long and I will not bore you, save to say that this poor 'demon' was of course a man of your race, dragged from his own world by our incantations and our diagrams and our crystals, and most anxious to return there."

"And did he return, lady?" Corum asked gently, for he saw that her eyes had a suggestion of tears in them. She shook her head.

"He could not, for we had no means of returning him. After the astonishment — for truly we had not really believed in our game! — we made him as comfortable here as we could, for we instantly felt sorry for what we had done when we realised that he was helpless. He learned something of our language and we learned something of his. We thought him very wise, though he insisted he was only a minor member of a large and not very important family of moderate nobility, that he was a soldier and not a scholar or a sorcerer. We understood his modesty but continued to admire him very much. I think he enjoyed that, although he continued to beg us to try to return him to his own age and his own plane."

Corum smiled. "I know how I should feel if two young girls had been responsible for tearing me suddenly away from all I knew and cared for and had then told me that they had only been playing a game and could not send me back!"

And the Lady Jane smiled in reply. "Aye. Well, by and by Gerane — that was one of his names — became reconciled to some degree and he and I fell in love and were happy for a short while. Sadly, I had not accounted for the fact that Aireda was also in love with Gerane." She sighed. "I had dreamed of being Guinevere, of Isolde, of other heroines of Romance, but I had forgotten that all these women were the victims of tragedy in the end. Our tragedy began to play itself out and at first I was not aware of it. Jealousy took power over Aireda and she grew to hate first me and then Gerane. She would plan revenges on us of varying sorts, but they were never completely satisfying to her. She had heard that Gerane's people had enemies — another race with bleaker souls — and she had guessed that one of her mother's rituals was to do with summoning members of this race — other demons, her mother had thought. Her first attempts were unsuccessful, but she absorbed herself in remembering every detail of those old spells."

"She conjured up Gerane's enemies?"

"Aye. Three of them came one night into the house. She was their first victim, for they hate humans as much as they hate elves — your folk. Shambling, awkward, poorly-fashioned creatures they were, completely unlike your folk, Prince Corum. We should call them trolls or some such name."

"And what did they do after they had slain Aireda?"

"She was not slain, but badly wounded, for it was in conversation with her later that I learned what she had done ..."

"And Gerane?"

"He had no sword. He had come with none. He had needed none in the Manor in the Forest."

"He was killed?"

"He heard the noise in the hall and came down to see what caused it. They butchered him there, by the door." She pointed. The tears shone on her cheeks now. "They cut him into sections, my elven love ..." She lowered her head.

Corum got up and went to comfort the old, beautiful Lady Jane Pentallyon. She gripped his mortal hand just once and had once again contained her grief. She straightened her back. "The — trolls — did not remain in the house. Doubtless they were confused by what had happened to them. They ran off into the night."

"Do you know what became of them?" Jhary asked.

"I heard several years later that beasts resembling men had begun to terrorise the folk of Exmoor and had eventually been taken and had stakes driven through their hearts, for they were thought to be the Devil's spawn. But the story spoke of only two, so perhaps one still lives in some lonely spot, still unaware of what had happened to him or where he is. I feel a certain sympathy for him ..."

"Do not grieve yourself, lady, by any further telling of this tale," said Corum gently.

"Since then," she went on, "I have concerned myself with the study of old wisdom. I learned something from Gerane and I have since spoken with various men and women who reckon themselves versed in the mystic arts. It was my hope to seek the plane of Gerane's people, but it is evident now that our planes are no longer in conjunction for I have learned enough to know that the planes circle as some say the planets circle about each other. I have learned a little of the art of seeing into the future and the past, into other planes, as Gerane's folk could ..."

"My folk also possess something of that art," said Corum in confirmation of her questioning glance, "but we have been losing it of late and can do nothing now beyond see into the five planes which comprise our Realm."

"Aye." She nodded. "I cannot explain why these powers wax and wane as they do."

"It is something to do with the gods," said Jhary. "Or our belief in them, perhaps."

"Your second sight gave you a glimpse into the future and that is how you knew we were seeking your help," Corum said.

Again she nodded.

"So you know that we are trying to return to our own age, where urgent deeds are necessary?"

"Aye."

"Can you help us?"

"I know of one who can put you on the road which leads to the achievement of that desire, but he can do no more."

"A sorcerer?"

"Of sorts. He, like you, is not of this age. Like you, he seeks constantly to return to his own world. He can move easily through the few centuries bordering this time, but he seeks to travel many millennia and that he cannot do."

"Is his name Bolorhiag?" asked Jhary suddenly. "An old man with a withered leg?"

"You describe the man, but to us he is known merely as the Friar, for he is inclined to wear clerical garb since this offers him the greatest protection in the periods of history he visits."

"It is Bolorhiag," said Jhary. "Another lost one. There are a few such souls who are whisked about the multiverse in this manner. Sometimes they are not at fault at all, but have been plucked, willy nilly, by whatever winds they are which blow through the dimensions. Others, like Bolorhiag, are experimenters — sorcerers, scientists, scholars, call them what you will — who have understood something of the nature of time and space but not enough to protect themselves. They, too, find themselves blown by those winds. There are also, as you know, ones like me who appear to be natural dwellers in the whole multiverse — or there are heroes, like yourself, Corum, who are doomed to move from age to age and plane to plane, from identity to identity, fighting for the Cause of Law. And there are women of a certain sort, like yourself, Lady Jane, who love these heroes. And there are malicious ones who hate them. What object there is to this myriad of existences I know not and it is probalby better that we know nothing of them …"

Lady Jane nodded gravely. "I think you are right, Sir Jhary, for the more one discovers the less point there seems in life at all. However, we are concerned not with philosophy but with immediate problems. I have sent out a summoning for the Friar and hope that he hears it and comes — it is not always the case. Meanwhile I have a gift for you, Prince Corum, for I feel that it may be useful to you. It appears that there is a mighty conjunction about to take place in the multiverse, when for a moment in time all ages and all planes will meet. I have never heard of such a thing before. That is part of my gift, the information. The other part is this …" From a thong around her neck she now drew out a slender object which though of a milky white colour also sparkled with every colour in the spectrum. It was a knife carved of a crystal which Corum had never seen before.

"Is it …?" he began.

She inclined her head to remove the thong. "It is the witch-knife which brought Gerane to me. It will, I think, bring aid to you when you need it greatly. It will call your brother to you …"

"My brother? I have no —"

"I was told this, she said. "And I can add nothing to it. But here is the witch-knife. Please take it."

Corum accepted it and placed the thong around his own neck. "Thank you, lady."

"Another will tell you when and how to use it, " she said. "And now, gentlemen, will you rest here at the Manor in the Forest, until such time as the Friar may present himself to us?"

"We would be honoured," said Corum. "But tell me, lady, if you know anything of the woman I love, for we are separated. I speak of the Lady Rhalina of Allomglyl and I fear much for her safety."

The Lady Jane frowned. "There was something concerning a woman which came momentarily into my head. I have the feeling that if you succeed in your present Quest, then you

82

will succeed in being reunited with her. If you fail, then you shall never see her again."

Corum's smile was grim.

"Then I must not fail," he said.

The Sixth Chapter

SALLING ON THE SEAS OF TIME

Three days went by and in normal circumstances Corum would have grown frustrated, impatient. But the old, beautiful lady calmed him, telling him something of the world she lived in but hardly ever saw. Some aspects of it were strange to him, but he began to understand why strange folk such as himself were, in the main, treated with suspicion, for what the Mabden of this world desired more than anything was equilibrium, stability not threatened by the doings of gods and demons and heroes, and he came to sympathise with them, though he felt that an understanding of what they feared would give them less to fear. They had invented for themselves a remote god whom they called simply The God and they had placed him far away from them. Some half-remembered fragments of the knowledge concerning the Cosmic Balance were theirs, and they had legends which might relate to the struggle between Law and Chaos. As he told the Lady Jane, all the Balance stood for was equilibrium — but stability could only be achieved by an understanding of the forces which were at work in the world, not a rejection of them.

On the third day one of the old retainers came running along the path up to the house where Jhary-a-Conel, Corum and the Lady Jane stood conversing. Speaking in his own language the man pointed into the forest.

"They still search for you, it seems, " she told them. "Your horses were released a day's ride away in order to put them off the scent and make them think you hid near Liskeard, but doubtless they come here because I am suspected a witch."

She smiled. "I deserve their suspicion far more than do the poor souls they sometimes catch and burn."

"Will they find us?"

"There is a place for you to hide. Others have been hidden there in the past. Old Kyn will take you there." She spoke to the old man and he nodded, grinning as if he enjoyed the excitement.

They were led into the attic of the house and there Old Kyn unlocked a false wall. Inside it was smoky and cramped but there was room to stretch and sleep if they wished to. They climbed into the darkness and Old Kyn replaced the false wall.

Some time later they heard voices, booted feet on the stairs. They pressed their backs against the false wall so that if it were thumped it would sound more solid. It was thumped, but it passed the inspection of the searchers whose coarse voices were grumbling and tired as if they had been at work ever since Corum and Jhary had escaped from the city.

The footsteps went away. Fainly they heard the jingle of harness, more voices, the sound of hoofs on the gravel and then silence.

A little later Old Kyn removed the false wall and leered into their hiding place. He winked. Corum grinned at him and climbed out, dusting down his scarlet robe. Jhary blew plaster from his cat's coat and began to stroke the little beast. He said something in Old Kyn's language which made the man wheeze with laughter.

Downstairs Lady Jane's face was serious. "I thing they will return," she said. "They noticed that our chapel has not been used for a good while."

"Your chapel?"

"Where we are meant to pray if we do not go to church. There are laws governing such things."

Corum shook his head in astonishment. "Laws?" He rubbed at his face. "This world is indeed hard to fathom."

"If the Friar does not come soon, you may have to leave here and seek fresh sanctuary," she said. "I have already sent for a friend who is a priest. Next time those soldiers come they shall find a very devout Lady Jane, I hope."

"Lady, I hope that you will not suffer for us," said Corum seriously.

"Worry not. There's little they can prove. When this fear dies down they will forget me again for a while."

"I pray it is true."

Corum went early to bed that night, for he felt unnaturally weary. The main fear was for Lady Jane and he could not help but feel she had made too little of the incident. At last he slept, but was awakened shortly after midnight.

It was Jhary and he was dressed, with his hat upon his head and his cat upon his shoulder. "The time has come," he said, "to come to time."

Corum rubbed at his eyes, not understanding the dandy's remark.

"Bolorhiag is here."

Corum swung himself from the bed. "I will dress and come down directly."

When he descended the stairs he saw that Lady Jane, wrapped in a dark cloak, her white hair unbound, stood there with Jhary-a-Conel and a small, wizened man who walked with the aid of a staff. The man's head was disproportionately large for his frail body which even the folds of his priest's gown could not hide. He was speaking in a high, querulous voice.

"I know you Timeras. You are a rogue."

"I am not Timeras in this identity, Bolorhiag. I am Jhary-a-Conel ..."

"But still a rogue. I resent even speaking the same tongue as you and only do so for the sake of the lovely Lady Jane."

"You are both rogues!" laughed the old, beautiful woman. "And you know that you cannot help but like each other."

"I only help him because you have asked me to do so," insisted the wizened man, "and because he may one day admit that he can help me."

"I have told you before, Bolorhiag, that I have much knowledge and hardly any skills. I would help you if I could, but my mind is a patchwork of memories — fragments of a thousand lives are in my skull. You should have sympathy for a wretch such as I."

"Bah!" Bolorhiag turned his twisted back and looked at Corum with his bright blue eyes. "And this is the other rogue, eh?"

Corum bowed.

"The Lady Jane requests me to ship you out of this age and into another where you will be less bothersome to her," Bolorhiag went on. "I will do it willingly, of course, for her heart is too kind for her own good. But I do no favours for you, young man, you understand."

"I understand, sir."

"Then let us get about it. The winds blow through and may be gone again before we can set our course. My carriage is outside."

Corum approached Lady Jane Pentallyon and took her hand, kissing it gently. "I thank you for this, my lady. I thank you for your hospitality, your confidence, your gifts and I pray that you will know happiness one day."

"Perhaps in another life," she said. "Thank you for such thoughts, and let me kiss you now." She bent and touched his forehead with her lips. "Farewell, my elven prince ..."

He turned away so that she would not see that he had noticed the tears in her eyes. He followed the wizened man as he hopped towards the door.

It was a small vessel he saw on the gravel outside the house. It was hardly large enough for three and had plainly been designed to take one in comfort. It had a high curved prow of a substance neither wood nor metal but much pitted and scored as if it had weathered many storms. A mast rose from the centre, though there was no sail furled on the yard.

"Sit there," said Bolorhiag impatiently, indicating the bench to his right. "I will sit between you and steer the craft."

After Corum had squeezed himself into place, Bolorhiag sat next to him and Jhary sat on the other side of the old man. A globe on a pivot seemed the only controls of the quaintly-shaped craft and now Bolorhiag raised his hand to salute the Lady Jane who stood in the shadows of the doorway, then took the globe between both palms.

Again Corum and Jhary bowed towards the door, but now the Lady Jane had disappeared altogether. Corum felt a tear form in his own good eye and he thought he knew why she did not watch them leave.

Suddenly something shimmered around the mast and Corum saw that it was a faint area of light shaped like a triangular sail. It grew stronger and stronger until it resembled an ordinary sail of cloth, bulging in a wind, though no wind blew.

Bolorhiag muttered to himself and the little craft seemed to move and yet did not move.

Corum glanced at the Manor in the Forest. It seemed framed in dancing brightness.

Daylight suddenly surrounded them. They saw figures outside the house, all around them, but the figures did not appear to see them. Horsemen — the soldiers who had searched the house the day before. They vanished. It was dark again and then light and then the house was gone and the boat rocked, turned, bounced.

"What is happening?" Corum cried out.

"What you wanted to happen, I gather," snapped Bolorhiag. "You are enjoying a short voyage upon the seas of time."

Everywhere now was what appeared to be clouds of dark grey. The sail continued to strain at the mast. The unfelt wind continued to blow. The boat moved on, with its inventor in his black robe muttering over his globe, steering it this way and that.

Sometimes the grey clouds would change colour, become green or blue or deep brown, and Corum would feel peculiar pressures upon him, find it difficult to breathe for a few moments, but the experience would quickly pass. Bolorhiag seemed completely oblivious of these sensations and even Jhary gave them no special attention. Once or twice the cat would give a faint cry and cling closer to its master, but that was the only sign that others felt the discomforts that Corum felt.

And then the ship's sail went limp and began to fade. Bolorhiag cursed in a harsh language of many consonants and spun the globe so that the ship whirled at a dizzying speed and Corum felt his stomach turn over.

Then the old man grunted in satisfaction as the sail reappeared and filled out again. "I thought we had lost the wind for good," he said. "There is nothing more aggravating than being becalmed on the time seas. Hardly anything more dangerous, either, if one is passing through some solid substance!" He laughed richly at this, nudging Jhary in the ribs. "You look ill, Timeras, you rogue."

"How long will this voyage last, Bolorhiag?" said Jhary in a strained voice.

"How long?" Bolorhiag stroked the globe, seeing something within it that they could not see. "What meaningless remark is that? You should know better, Timeras!"

"I should have known better than to begin on this voyage. I suspect you of becoming senile, old man."

"After several thousand years I am bound to begin to feel my years." The old man grinned wickedly at Jhary's consternation.

The speed of the ship seemed to increase.

"Stand by to turn about! shouted Bolorhiag, apparently quite mad, almost hysterical. "Ready to drop anchor, lads! Date ahoy!"

The ship swung as if caught by a powerful current. The peculiar sail sagged and vanished. The grey light began to grow brighter.

The ship stood upon an expanse of dark rock overlooking a green valley far, far below.

Bolorhiag began to chuckle as he saw their expressions. "I have few pleasures," he said, "but my favourite is to terrify my passengers. It is, in part, what I regard as my just payment. I am not mad, I think, gentlemen. I am merely desperate."

The Seventh Chapter

THE LAND OF TALL STONES

Bolorhiag allowed them to disembark from his tiny craft. Corum looked around him at the rather bleak landscape. Everywhere he looked he saw in the distance tall columns of stone, sometimes standing singly, sometimes in groups. The stone varied in colour but had plainly been put there by some intelligence.

"What are they?" he asked.

Bolorhiag shrugged. "Stones. The inhabitants of these parts raise them."

"For what purpose?"

"For the same purpose that makes them dig deep holes in the ground — you will discover those as well — to pass the time. They cannot explain it any other way. I understand that it is their art. No better or worse than much of the art one sees."

"I suppose so," said Corum doubtfully. "And now perhaps you will explain, Master Bolorhiag, why we have been brought here."

"This age corresponds roughly with the age of your own Fifteen Planes. The conjunction comes soon and you are better here than elsewhere. There is a building which is occasionally seen here and which has the name in some parts of the Vanishing Tower. It comes and goes through the planes. Timeras here knows the story, I am sure."

Jhary nodded. "I know it. But this is dangerous, Bolorhiag. We could enter the Vanishing Tower and never return. You are aware that —?"

"I am aware of most things about the tower, but you have little choice. It is your only means of getting back to your own age and your own plane, believe me. I know of no other method. You must risk the dangers."

Jhary shrugged. "As you say. We will risk them."

"Here." Bolorhiag offered him a rolled sheet of parchment. "It is a map of how to get there from here. A rather rough map, I am afraid. Geography was never my strong point."

"We are most grateful to you, Master Bolorhiag," Corum said gracefully.

"I want no gratitude, but I do want information. I am some ten thousand years away from my own age and wonder what barrier it is which allows me to cross it one way but not the other. If you should ever discover a clue to the answer to this question and if you, Timeras, ever pass through this age and plane again, I should want to hear of it."

"I will make a point of it, Bolorhiag."

"Then farewell, both of you."

The old man hunched himself once more over his steering crystal. Once more the peculiar sail appeared and filled with the unfelt wind. And then the little ship and its occupant had faded.

Corum stared thoughtfully at the huge, mysterious stones.

Jhary had unrolled the map. "We must climb down this cliff until we reach the valley," he said. "Come, Prince Corum, we had best start now."

They found the least steep part of the cliff and began to inch their way down it.

They had not gone very far when they heard a shout above them and looked up. It was the little wizened man and he was hopping up and down on his stick. "Corum! Timeras or whatever pseudonym you're using! Wait!"

"What is it, Master Bolorhiag?"

"I forgot to tell you, Prince Corum, that if you find yourself in extreme danger or distress within the next day — and only the next day — go to a point where you see a storm which is isolated. Do you hear?"

"I hear. But what —?"

"I cannot repeat myself, the time tide changes. Enter the storm and take out the witch-knife given you by the Lady Jane. Hold it so that it traps the lightning. Then call upon the name of Elric of Melnibone and say that he must come to make the Three Who Are One — the Three Who Are One. Remember that. You are part of the same thing. It will be all you need to do for the Third — the Many-named Hero — will be drawn to the Two."

"Who told you all this, Master Bolorhiag?" Jhary called, clinging to the rock of the cliff and not looking down.

"Oh, a creature. It does not matter who told me. But you must remember that, Prince Corum. The storm — the knife — the incantation. Remember it!"

Corum called, half to humour the old man, "I will remember."

"Farewell, again." And Bolorhiag stepped back from the cliff-top and was gone.

They climbed down in silence, too intent on finding holds in the rockface to discuss Bolorhiag's peculiar message.

And when, eventually, they reached the floor of the valley, they were too exhausted to speak, but lay still, looking up at the great sky.

Later Corum said: "Did you understand the old man's words, Jhary?"

Jhary shook his head. "The Three Who Are One. It sounds ominous. I wonder if it has any connection with what we saw in Limbo?"

"Why should it?"

"I know not. Just a thought which popped into my brain because it was empty. We had best forget that for a while and hope to discover the Vanishing Tower. Bolorhiag was right. The map *is* crude."

"And what is the Vanishing Tower?"

"It once existed in your own Realm, Corum, I believe — in one of the five planes, but not yours. On the edge of a place called Balwyn Moor in a valley much like this one which was called Darkvale. Chaos was fighting Law and winning in those days. It came against Darkvale and its keep — a small castle, rather than a tower. The knight of the keep sought the aid of the Lords of Law and they granted that aid, enabling him to move his tower into another dimension. But Chaos had gained great power then and cursed the tower, decreeing that it should shift for all time, never staying more than a few hours on any one plane. And so it shifts to this day. The original knight — who was protecting a fugitive from Chaos — was soon insane, as was the fugitive. Then came Voilodion Ghagnasdiak to the Vanishing Tower and there he remains."

"Who is he?"

"An unpleasant creature. Trapped in the tower now and fearing to step outside, he uses the tower to lure the unsuspecting to him. He keeps them there until they bore him and then he slays them."

"And that is whom we must fight when we enter the Vanishing Tower?"

"Exactly."

"Well, there are two of us and we are armed."

"Voilodion Ghagnasdiak is very powerful — a sorcerer of no mean skill."

"Then we cannot conquer him! My hand and eye no longer come to my assistance."

Jhary shrugged. He stroked his cat's chin. "Aye. I said it was dangerous, but as Bolorhiag pointed out, we have little choice, have we? After all, we are still on our way to find Tanelorn. I am beginning to feel that my sense of direction returns. We are nearer Tanelorn now than we have been before."

"How do you know?"

"I know. I know, that is all."

Corum sighed. "I am weary of mysteries, of sorceries, of tragedies. I am a simple ..."

"No time for self-pity, Prince Corum. Come, this is the way we want to go."

They followed a roaring river upstream for two miles. The river rushed through a steep valley and they climbed along the sloping sides, using the trees to stop them from falling down into the white rapids. Then they came to a place where the river forked and Jhary pointed to a place where it was shallow, running over pebbles. "A ford. We need yonder island. That is where the Vanishing Tower will appear, when it appears."

"Will we wait long?"

"I do not know. Still the island looks as if it has game on it and the river has fish in it. We shall not starve while we wait."

"I think of Rhalina, Jhary — not to mention the fate of Bro-an-Vadhagh and Lywm-an-Esh. I grow impatient."

"Our only means of getting back to the Fifteen Planes is to enter the Vanishing Tower. Thus, we must await the pleasure of the tower."

Corum shrugged and began to wade through the ice-cold stream towards the island.

Suddenly Jhary shouted and pushed past Corum. "It is there! It is there already! Quickly, Corum!"

He ran to where a stone keep stood above the trees. It seemed an ordinary sort of tower. Corum could hardly believe that this was their goal.

"Soon we shall see Tanelorn!" cried Jhary jubilantly. He reached the other side of the island, with Corum running some distance behind him, and began to crash through the undergrowth.

There was a doorway at the base of the keep and it was open.

"Come, Corum!"

Jhary was almost inside the door now. Corum went more warily, remembering what he had heard of Voilodion Ghagnasdiak, the dweller in the tower. But Jhary, his cat as ever upon his shoulder, had gone through the door.

Corum broke into a run, his hand on his sword hilt. He reached the tower.

The door closed suddenly. He heard Jhary's yell of horror from within. He clung to the wood of the door, he beat on it.

Inside Jhary was calling: "Find the Three Who Are One whatever it is. It is our only hope now, Corum! Find the Three Who Are One!" There came a chuckle which was not Jhary's.

"Open!" roared Corum. "Open your damned door!"

But the door would not budge.

The chuckle was fat and warm. It grew louder and Corum could not longer hear Jhary's voice at all. The fat, warm voice said:

"Welcome to the home of Voilodion Ghagnasdiak, friend. You are an honoured guest."

Corum felt something happen to the tower. He looked back. The forest was disappearing. He clung to the handle, kept his feet on the step for a moment. His body was racked by painful spasms, one following closely upon the other. Every tooth in his head ached, every bone in his body throbbed.

And then he had lost his grip upon the tower and saw it vanish away. He fell.

He fell and landed on wet, marshy ground. It was night. Somewhere a dark bird hooted.

The Eighth Chapter

INTO THE SMALL STORM

Daybreak found Corum walking. His feet were weary and he was lost, but still he walked. He could think of nothing else to do and he felt bound to do something. Marshland stretched everywhere. Marsh birds rose in flocks into the red morning sky. Marsh animals slithered or hopped across the wet ground in search of food.

Corum selected another clump of reeds and made it his goal.

When he reached the clump of reeds he paused for a moment and then fixed his eye on another clump and began to make for that.

And so he progressed.

He was desolate. He had lost Rhalina. Now he had lost Jhary and thus his hope of finding either Rhalina or Tanelorn. And so he had lost Bro-an-Vadhagh and Lywm-an-Esh and he had lost them to conquering Chaos, to Glandyth-a-Krae.

All lost.

"All lost," he murmured through his numbed lips.

"All lost."

The marsh birds cackled and screeched. The marsh animals scuttled through the reeds, unseen as they ran on hasty errands.

Was this whole world a marsh? It seemed so. Marsh upon marsh.

He reached the next clump of reeds and he sat down on the damp ground, looking at the wide sky, the red clouds, the emerging sun. It was getting hot.

Steam began to rise over the marsh.

Corum took off his helmet. His silver greaves were grimed with mud, his hands were filthy — even the six-fingered Hand of Kwll was coated in mire.

Steam moved slowly over the marsh as if seeking something. He wet his face and lips with the brackish water, tempted to remove his scarlet robe and his silver byrnie and yet, for the moment, preferring their security should he be attacked by a larger marsh dweller than any he had so far seen.

Steam was everywhere. In places the mud bubbled and spat. The hot, damp air began to pain his throat and lungs and his eyelids became heavy as a great weariness came over him.

And it seemed to him that he saw a figure moving through the steam. A tall figure wading slowly through the boiling mud. A giant who dragged something heavy behind it. His head dropped to his chest and he raised it with difficulty. He no longer saw the figure. He realised that some marsh gas was making him drowsy, making him hallucinate.

He rubbed at his eyes but only succeeded in making his mortal eye fill with mud.

And then he felt a presence behind him.

He turned.

Something loomed there, as white and intangible as the steam. Something fell upon him, entangling his arms and legs. He tried to draw his sword but he could not free himself. He was carried upwards and other creatures struggled near by, snapping and shouting. The heat began to disperse and then it was terribly cold, so cold that all the other creatures were suddenly silent. Then it was dark.

And then it was wet. He spat salt water from his mouth and cursed. He was free again and he felt soft sand beneath his feet and he waded waist-deep through the water, the silver helm still clutched in his hand, and fell upon a dark yellow beach, gasping.

Corum thought he knew what had happened to him, but he found it hard to believe. For the third time he had seen the mysterious Wading God and for the third time the gigantic fisherman had influenced his destiny — first by hurling him upon the coast of the Ragha-da-Kheta, second by bring Jhary-a-Conel to Moidel's Mount, and third by saving him from the marsh world — a world, it now appeared, which must be on one of the Fifteen Planes — as this new world must be.

If it were a new world, of course, and not merely part of the same one.

Whichever it was, it was an improvement. He began to pick himself up.

And he saw the old woman standing there. She was a dumpy little woman and her red face was at once frightened and prim. She was soaking wet and wringing out her bonnet with her hands.

"Who are you?" Corum said.

"Who are you, young man? I was walking along the beach minding my own business when this terrible wave suddenly appeared and completely drenched me. It is none of your doing, is it?"

"I hope not, ma'am."

"Are you some mariner, then, who has been shipwrecked?"

"That is the truth of it," Corum agreed. "Tell me, ma'am, where is this land?"

"You are near the fishing town of Chynezh Port, young sir. Up there," she pointed up the cliffs, "lies the great Balwyn Moor and then ..."

"Balwyn Moor. Beyond it lies Darkvale, eh?"

The old woman pursed her lips. "Aye. Darkvale. None visits it these days, however."

"But that is the place of the Vanishing Tower?"

"So 'tis said."

"Is it possible to purchase a horse in Chynezh Port?"

"I suppose so. The horse-breeders of Balwyn Moor are famous and they bring some of their best to Chynezh for the foreign trade — or did before the fighting."

"There is a war taking place?"

"Call it that. Things came out of the sea and attacked our

95

boats. We have heard that folk have suffered much worse elsewhere and that we are relatively safe from the most dreadful of these monsters. But we lost half our menfolk and now none dares fish and, of course, no foreign ships put into our harbour to buy horses."

"So Chaos returns here, too," mused Corum. He sighed.

"You must aid me, old woman," he told her. "For I may in turn aid you and make these seas safe again. Now — the horse."

She led him along the beach and round a cliff and he saw a pleasant fishing town with a good, strong harbour and in the harbour were all their boats, their sails tightly furled.

"You see," she said. "Unless the boats go out again soon we of Chynezh Port shall starve, for fish is our livelihood."

"Aye." Corum put his mortal hand upon her shoulder. "Now, take me to where I can purchase a steed."

She led him to a stables on the outskirts of the town, near the road which wound up the cliff towards the moor. Here a peasant sold him a pair of horses, one white and one black, almost twins, with all the necessary gear. Corum had taken it into his head that he would need two horses, though he hardly knew why.

Riding the white horse and leading the black one, he began to ascend the winding road, making for Darkvale under the puzzled gaze of the old woman and the peasant. He reached the top and saw that the road went on along the cliff until it disappeared into a wooded dale. The day was warm and pleasant and it was hard to believe that this world was threatened by Chaos too. It was very much like his own land of Bro-an-Vadhagh and parts of the coastline even seemed half-familiar.

He became filled with a sense of anticipation as he entered the wood and listened to the birdsong in the trees. It was very peaceful and yet something seemed strange. He slowed his horses to a walk, proceeding almost hesitantly.

And then he saw it ahead.

A black cloud on the road through the trees. A cloud which began to grumble with thunder and flash with lightning.

Corum reined in his horses and dismounted. From the neck of his byrnie he pulled out the crystal witch-knife which the Lady Jane had given him. He strove to remember Bolorhiag's shouted words. *Go to the point where you see a storm which is isolated. Take out the witch-knife given you by the Lady Jane. Hold it so that it traps the lightning. Then call upon the name of Elric of Melnibone and say that he must come to make the Three Who Are One ... You are part of the same thing ... the Third — the Many-named Hero — will be drawn to the Two ...*

"Well," he said to himself, "there is nothing else for it. In truth I'll need allies to go against Voilodion Ghagnasdiak in his Vanishing Tower. And if these allies are powerful, then so much the better."

With the crystal witch-knife held aloft he stepped into the roaring cloud.

Lightning struck the witch-knife and filled him with shivering energy. All about him was disturbance and noise. He opened his mouth and he cried:

"Elric of Melnibone! You must come to make the Three Who Are One! Elric of Melnibone! You must come to make the Three Who Are One! Elric of Melnibone!"

And then a fierce bolt of lightning came down and shattered the witch-knife, flung Corum down to the ground. Voices seemed to wail across the world, winds swept in all directions. He staggered upright wondering suddenly if he had been betrayed. He could see nothing but the lightning, hear nothing but the thunder.

He fell and struck his head. He began to raise himself to his feet.

And then mellow light filled the forest once more and the birds sang.

"The storm. It has gone." He looked about him and then he saw the man who lay on the grass. He recognised him. It was the man he had seen fighting on dragon-back when he hung in Limbo. "And you? Are you called Elric of Melnibone?"

The albino got to his feet. His crimson eyes were full of a permanent sorrow. He answered politely enough.

"I am Elric of Melnibone. Are you to thank for rescuing me from those creatures Theleb K'aarna summoned?"

Corum shook his head. Elric was dressed in a travel-stained shirt and breeks of black silk. There were black boots on his feet and a black belt around his waist which supported a black scabbard into which the albino sheathed a huge black broadsword carved from hilt to tip with peculiar runes. Over all this black was drawn a voluminous cloak of white silk with a large hood attached to it. Elric's milk-white hair seemed to flow over the cloak and blend with it.

"'Twas I that summoned you," Corum admitted, "but I know of no Theleb K'aarna. I was told that I had only one opportunity to receive your aid and that I must take it in this particular place at this particular time. I am called Corum Jhaelen Irsei — the Prince in the Scarlet Robe — and I ride upon a Quest of grave import."

Elric was frowning and looking about him. "Where is this forest?"

"It is is nowhere on your plane or in your time, Prince Elric. I summoned you to aid me in my battle against the Lords of Chaos. Already I have been instrumental in destroying two of the Sword Rulers — Arioch and Xiombarg — but the third, the most powerful, remains ..."

"Arioch of Chaos — and Xiombarg?" The albino looked unconvinced. "You have destroyed two of the most powerful members of the Company of Chaos? Yet but a month since I spoke with Arioch. He is my patron ..."

Corum realised that Elric was not as familiar as he with the structure of the multiverse. "There are many planes of existence," he said as gently as he could. "In some the Lords of Chaos are strong. In some they are weak. In some, I have heard, they do not exist at all. You must accept that here Arioch and Xiombarg have been banished so that effectively they no longer exist in my world. It is the third of the Sword Rulers who threatens us now — the strongest. King Mabelode."

The albino was frowning and Corum feared that the wilful prince would choose not to aid him after all. "In my — plane — Mabelode is no stronger than Arioch and Xiombarg. This makes a travesty of all my understanding ..."

Corum drew a deep breath. "I will explain," he said, "as much as I can. For some reason Fate has selected me to be the hero who must banish the domination of Chaos from the Fifteen Planes of Earth. I am at present travelling on my way to seek a city which we call Tanelorn, where I hope to find aid. But my guide is a prisoner in a castle close to here and before I can continue I must rescue him. I was told how I might summon aid to — help me effect this rescue ... And I used the spell to bring you to me. I —" Corum hesitated a fraction of a second, for he knew that Bolorhiag had not told him this and yet he knew it was the truth he spoke — "was to tell you that if you aided me, then you would aid yourself — that if I was successful then you would receive something which would make your task easier …"

"Who told you this?"

"A wise man."

Corum watched the puzzled albino go and sit down upon a tree-trunk and place his head in his hands. "I have been drawn away at an unfortunate time," said Elric. "I pray that you speak the truth to me, Prince Corum." Suddenly he looked up and fixed Corum with those strange, crimson eyes. "It is a marvel that you speak at all — or at least that I understand you. How can this be?"

"I was — informed that we should be able to communicate easily — because 'we are part of the same thing'. Do not ask me to explain more, Prince Elric, for I know no more."

"Well this may be an illusion. I may have killed myself or become digested by that machine of Theleb K'aarna's, but plainly I have no choice but to agree to aid you in the hope that I am, in turn, aided." The albino glanced hard at Corum.

Corum went to get the horses where he had left them further up the road. He returned with them as the albino stood up, his hands on his hips, staring around him. He knew what it was to be plunged suddenly into a new world and he sympathised with the Melnibonean. He handed the black horse's reins to Elric and the albino climbed into the saddle and stood upright in the stirrups for a moment as he got the feel of the trappings, for he was plainly not used to the particular kind of saddle and stirrup.

They began to ride.

"You spoke of Tanelorn," said Elric. "It is for the sake of Tanelorn that I find myself in this dreamworld of yours."

Corum was astonished at Elric's casual mention of Tanelorn. "You know where Tanelorn lies?"

"In my own world, aye — but why should it lie in this one?"

"Tanelorn lies in all planes, though in different guises. There is one Tanelorn and it is eternal with many forms."

The two men continued to make their way through the forest as they spoke. Corum could hardly believe that Elric was real — just as Elric could hardly believe, it seemed, that this world was real. The albino rubbed his face several times and peered hard at Corum.

"Where go we now?" asked Elric finally. "To the castle?"

Corum spoke hesitantly, remembering Bolorhiag's words. "First we must have the Third Hero — the Many-Named Hero."

"And you will summon him with sorcery, too?"

Corum shook his head. "I was told not. I was told that he would meet us — drawn from whichever Age he exists in by the necessity to complete the Three Who Are One."

"What mean these phrases? What is the Three Who Are One?"

"I know little more than you, friend Elric, save that it will need all three of us to defeat he who holds my guide prisoner."

Now they came to Balwyn Moor, leaving the forest behind them. On one side were the cliffs and the sea and the world was silent and at rest so that any threat from Chaos seemed very distant.

"Your gauntlet is of curious manufacture," Elric said.

Corum laughed. "So thought a doctor I lately encountered. He believed it was a man-made limb. But it is said to have belonged to a god — one of the Lost Gods who mysteriously left the world millennia ago. Once it had special properties, just as this eye did. It could see into a netherworld — a terrible place from where I could sometimes draw aid."

"All you tell me makes the complicated sorceries and cosmologies of my world seem simple in comparison."

"It only seems complicated because it is strange," Corum answered. "Your world would doubtless seem incomprehensible to me if I were suddenly flung into it." Corum broke into laughter again. "Besides, this particular plane is not my world, either, though it resembles it more than do many. We have one thing in common, Elric, and that is that we are both doomed to play a role in the constant struggle between the Lords of the Higher Worlds — and we shall never understand why that struggle takes place, why it is eternal. We fight, we suffer agonies of mind and soul, but we are never sure that our suffering is worthwhile."

Elric plainly agreed completely. "You are right. We have much in common, you and I, Corum."

Corum looked down the road and there was a mounted man sitting stock still in his saddle. The warrior seemed to be waiting for them.

"Perhaps this is the Third of whom Bolorhiag spoke," said Corum as they slowed their pace and began, cautiously, to approach the warrior.

He was jet black with a huge, heavy, handsome head covered by the snarling mask of a snarling bear, its pelt going down his back. The mask could be used for a visor, Corum thought, but was now pushed off the face armour which was also black and, like Elric, he had a great black-hilted sword in a black scabbard. The pair of them made Corum feel almost gaudy in comparison. The black warrior's horse was not black — it was a strong, tall roan, a war horse. Hanging from his saddle was a great round shield.

The man did not seem pleased to see them. Rather he was horrified.

"I know you! I know you both!" he gasped.

Corum had never seen the man before and yet he, too, felt recognition.

"How came you here to Balwyn Moor, friend?" he asked.

The black warrior licked his lips, his eyes almost glazed. "Balwyn Moor? This is Balwyn Moor? I have been here but a few moments. Before that I was — I was ... Ah! The memory starts to fade again." He pressed one massive black hand to his brow. "A name — another name! No more! Elric! Corum! But I — I am now ..."

"How do you know our names?" cried Elric, aghast.

The man replied in a whisper. "Because — don't you see? — I am Elric — I am Corum — oh, this is the worst agony ... Or, at least, I have been or am to be Elric and Corum..."

Corum was sympathetic. He remembered what Jhary had told him of the Champion Eternal. "Your name, sir?"

"A thousand names are mine. A thousand heroes I have been. Ah! I am — I am — John Daker — Erekosë — Urlik — many, many, many more ... The memories, the dreams, the existences." He stared at them suddenly through his pain-filled eyes. "Do you not understand? Am I the only one to be doomed to understand? I am he who has been called the Champion Eternal — I am the hero who has existed forever — and, yes, I am Elric of Melnibone — Prince Corum Jhaelen Irsei — I am you, also. We three are the same creature and a myriad other creatures besides. We three are one thing —

101

doomed to struggle forever and never understand why. Oh! My head pounds. Who tortures me so? Who?"

From beside Corum Elric spoke. "You say you are another incarnation of myself?"

"If you would phrase it so! You are both other incarnations of *myself!*"

"So," Corum said, "that is what Bolorhiag meant by the Three Who Are One. We are all aspects of the same man, yet we have tripled our strength because we have been drawn from three different ages. It is the only power which might successfully go against Voilodion Ghagnasdiak of the Vanishing Tower."

Elric spoke quietly. "Is that the castle wherein your guide is imprisoned?"

"Aye." Corum took a stronger grip on the reins. "The Vanishing Tower flickers from one plane to another, from one age to another, and exists in a single location only for a few moments at a time. But because we are three separate incarnations of a single hero it is possible that we form a sorcery of some kind which will enable us to follow the tower and attack it. Then, if we free my guide, we can continue on to Tanelorn ..."

The black warrior raised his head, hope beginning to replace despair. "Tanelorn? I, too, seek Tanelorn. Only there may I discover some remedy to my dreadful fate — which is to know all previous incarnations and be hurled at random from one existence to another! Tanelorn — I must find her!"

"I too, must discover Tanelorn." The albino seemed half-amused, as if beginning to enjoy the strange situation. "For on my own plane her inhabitants are in great danger."

"So we have a common purpose as well as a common identity," said Corum. Perhaps now there was some chance of saving Jhary and finding Thalina. "Therefore we shall fight in concert, I pray. First we must free my guide, then go on to Tanelorn."

The black giant growled: "I'll aid you willingly."

Corum bowed his head in thanks. "And what shall we call you — you who are ourselves?"

"Call me Erekosë — though another name suggests itself to me— for it was as Erekosë that I came closest to knowing forgetfulness and the fullfilment of love."

"Then you are to be envied, Erekosë," Elric said. "For at least you have come close to forgetfulness ..."

The black giant shook his reins and fell in beside Corum. He gave Elric a sideways stare and his mouth was crooked. "You have no inkling of what it is I must forget." He turned to the Prince in the Scarlet Robe. "Now Corum — which way to the Vanishing Tower?"

"This road leads to it. We ride down now to Darkvale, I believe."

With a man who was a shadow of himself on either side of him, with a sense of doom filling his mind when it should have begun to feel hope, Corum guided his horse down towards Darkvale.

BOOK THREE

In which Prince Corum discovers far more than Tanelorn

The First Chapter

VOILODION GHAGNASDIAK

Now the road narrowed and became much steeper. Corum saw it disappear into the black shadows between two high cliffs and he knew that he had come to Darkvale.

He felt ill at ease still, with the two men who were himself, and he fought not to brood upon the implications of what all this meant. He pointed down the hill and spoke as lightly as possible.

"Darkvale." He looked at the albino face on one side of him, the jet black face on the other. Both were grim and set. "I am told there was a village here once. An uninviting spot, eh — brothers ..."

"I have seen worse." Erekosë clapped his legs hard against his horse's sides. "Come, let's get all this done with ..." He spurred the roan ahead and galloped wildly down towards the gap in the cliffs.

Corum followed him more slowly and Elric was the slowest of all. As he rode into the darkness, Corum looked up. The cliffs came so close together at the top that they met, cutting off all but a little light. And at the foot of the cliffs were ruins — what was left of the Town of Darkvale before Chaos came against it. The ruins were all twisted and warped as if they had become liquid and then turned solid again. Corum searched for the most likely spot where he would find the Vanishing Tower and at last he came to a pit which seemed freshly dug. He inspected it closely. It was of a size with the Vanishing Tower. "Here is where we must wait," he said.

Elric joined him. "What must we wait for, friend Corum?"

"For the Tower. I would guess that this is where it appears when it is in this plane."

"And when will it appear?"

"At no particular time. We must wait. And then, as soon as we see it we must rush it and attempt to enter before it vanishes again, moving on to the next plane."

Corum looked for Erekosë. The black giant was sitting on the ground with his back against a slab of the twisted rock. Elric approached him.

"You seem more patient than I, Erekosë."

"I have learned patience, for I have lived since time began and will live on at the end of time."

Elric loosened his horse's girth strap, calling out to Corum. "Who told you that the Tower would appear here?"

"A sorcerer who doubtless serves Law as I do, for I am a mortal doomed to battle Chaos."

"As am I," said Erekosë.

"As am I," said the albino, "though I'm sworn to serve it." He shrugged and looked strangely at the other two. Corum guessed what he was thinking. "And why do you seek Tanelorn, Erekosë?"

Erekosë stared up at the crack of light where the cliffs met. "I have been told that I may find peace there —— and wisdom —— a means of returning to the world of the Eldren where dwells the woman I love, for it has been said that since Tanelorn exits in all planes at all times it is easier for a man who dwells there to pass between the planes, discover the particular one he seeks. What interest have you in Tanelorn, Lord Elric?"

"I know Tanelorn and I know that you are right to seek it. My mission seems to be the defence of that city upon my own plane —— but even now my friends may be destroyed by that which has been brought against them. I pray Corum is right and that in the Vanishing Tower I shall find a means to defeat Theleb K'aarna's beasts and their masters ..."

Corum raised his jewelled hand to his jewelled eye. "I seek Tanelorn for I have heard the city can aid me in my struggle against Chaos." He said no more of Arkyn's whispered instructions so long ago in the Temple of Law.

"But Tanelorn," Elric told him, "will fight neither Law nor Chaos. That is why she exists for eternity."

Corum had heard as much from Jhary. "Aye," he said. "Like Erekosë I do not seek swords, but wisdom."

When night came the three took turns to stand watch, occasionally conversing, but more often than not merely sitting or standing and staring at the place where the Vanishing Tower might appear.

Corum found his two companions rather heavy company

after Jhary and he felt a certain dislike for them, perhaps because they were so much like himself.

But then at dawn while Erekosë nodded and Elric slept soundly, the air shuddered and Corum saw the familiar outlines of Voilodion Ghagnasdiak's tower begin to grow solid.

"It is here!" he shouted. Erekosë sprang up at once but Elric was only just stirring. "Hasten Elric!"

Now Elric joined them and he, like Erekosë, had his black sword in his hand. The swords were almost brothers —— both black, both terrible in aspect, both carved with runes.

Corum was ahead of the others, determined not to be shut out this time. He ran into the dark doorway and was at first blinded, shouting for his friends to join him. "Hasten! Hasten!"

Corum ran into a small antechamber and saw that reddish light illuminated the room, spilling from a great oil lamp which hung in chains from the ceiling. But then the door closed suddenly behind them and Corum knew they were trapped, prayed that they three would be powerfull enough to resist the sorcerer. His eye caught a movement at the slit window in the wall. Darkvale had gone and there was nothing but blue sea where it had been. The tower was already moving. He pointed it out silently to his companions.

Then he raised his head and yelled:

"Jhary! Jhary-a-Conel!"

Was the dandy dead? He prayed that he was not.

He listened carefully and heard a tiny noise which might have been a reply.

"Jhary!"

Corum motioned with his long, strong sword.

"Voilodion Ghagnasdiak? Am I to be thwarted? Have you left this place?"

"I have not left it. What do you want with me?"

Corum looked towards the next room, beneath a pointed arch. He led the way forward.

Brightness like the golden brightness he had seen in Limbo flickered and framed the humpen shape of Voilodion Ghagnasdiak —— a dwarf, overdressed in silks, ermine and satin, a miniature sword clutched in his coarse hand, a handsome head upon his tiny shoulders, bright eyes beneath thick black brows which met in the middle, a grin of welcome like the grin of a wolf. "At last someone new to relieve my ennui. But

109

lay down your swords, gentlemen, I beg you, for you are to be my guests."

"I know what fate your guests may expect," Corum said. "Know this, Voilodion Ghagnasdiak, we have come to release Jhary-a-Conel whom you hold prisoner. Give him up to us and we will not harm you."

The dwarf's handsome features grinned impishly back at Corum. "But I am very powerful. You cannot defeat me." He opened his arms. "Watch."

Waving his sword he made more lightning flash here and there in the room and forced Elrich to half-raise his sword as if it attacked him. Plainly this made him feel foolish and he stepped towards the dwarf. "Know this, Voilodion Ghagnasdiak, I am Elric of Melnibone and I have much power. I bear the Black Sword and it thirsts to drink your soul unless you release Prince Corum's friend!"

The dwarf's mirth was not abated. "Swords? What power have they?"

Erekosë growled: "Our swords are not ordinary blades. And we have been brought here by forces you could not comprehend —— wrenched from our own ages by the power of the gods themselves —— specifically to demand that this Jhary-a-Conel be given up to us."

"You are deceived," said Voilodion Ghagnasdiak, addressing all three. "Or you seek to deceive me. This Jhary is a witty fellow, I'd agree, but what interest could gods have in him?"

The albino impulsively raised his great black sword and Corum heard a sound like a moan of bloodlust come from it. He thought the sword an unhealthy weapon to bear.

But then Elrich was hurtling backwards, his sword flying from his grip. Voilodion Ghagnasdiak had merely bounced a yellow ball off his forehead —— but it had been powerful.

Corum let Erekosë go to Elric's aid while he kept his attention on the sorcerer, but as soon as Elric was on his feet Voilodion hurled another ball and this time the black sword deflected it so that it bounced harmlessly towards the far wall and then exploded. The heat seared their faces and the blast knocked the wind from them. Corum saw a blackness begin to writhe from the fire left behind by the explosion.

Voilodion Ghagnasdiak spoke equably enough. "It is dangerous to destroy the globes," he said, "for now what is in them will destroy you."

The black thing increased its size and the flame disappeared.

"I am free."

The voice came from the writhing shadow.

Voilodion Ghagnasdiak chuckled. "Aye. Free to kill these fools who reject my hospitality!"

"Free to be slain!" Elric cried impetuously.

Corum stared in terrified fascination as the thing began to grow like flowing, sentient hair which then slowly compressed and became a creature with a tiger's head, a gorilla's body and a hide as coarse as that of a rhinoceros. Black wings sprouted on its back and these flapped rapidly as it shifted its grip on its weapon —— a long, scythe-like thing which lashed out at the nearest man, the albino.

Corum moved to help Elric, remembering that Elric might be relying on him to use the power of the hand and the eye. He shouted: "My eye will not see into the netherworld. I cannot summon help."

But then Corum saw one of the yellow balls coming at him and another being flung at Erekosë. Both managed to deflect them so that they landed on the ground and burst. More winged monsters emerged and soon Corum had no time to think of aiding Elric, for he was concerned with fighting for his own life, ducking the whistling scythe as it sought to decapitate him.

Several times Corum managed to get under the monster's guard, but even when he did the thick skin turned his thrusts. And the beast moved quickly —— far faster than it would seem it could. Sometimes it would leap into the air, hovering on its wings before sweeping down on Corum again.

The Prince in the Scarlet Robe began to think that he had been deceived by Chaos into coming here, for the other two were as helpless against the monsters as was he.

He cursed himself for overconfidence and wished that they had formed a more coherent plan before rushing into the Vanishing Tower.

And over the sound of battle came the screeches of Voilodion Ghagnasdiak as he threw more of the yellow spheres into the room and they burst and more tiger-headed monsters formed in the air and pressed into the fray. The three men found themselves pushed back to the far wall.

"I fear I have summoned you two to your destruction."

111

Corum was panting and his sword arm was weary. "I had no warning that our powers would be so limited here. The tower must shift so fast that even the ordinary laws of sorcery do not apply within its walls."

Elric defended himself as two scythes swung at him at the same time. They seem to work well enough for the dwarf! If I could slay but a single ..."

One of the scythes drew blood and another ripped the albino's cloak. Yet another slashed his arm. Corum tried to help him, but a blade ripped his silver byrnie and another nicked his ear. He saw Elric stab a tiger-monster in the throat without seeming to harm the beast at all. He heard Elric's sword howl as if in fury at being thwarted of its prey.

Then Corum saw Elric grab a scythe from the hands of the tiger-thing and reverse it. The albino stabbed the monster in the chest and then blood spurted in earnest and the thing screamed as it was mortally wounded.

"I was right!" called the Prince of Melnibone. "Only their own weapons can harm them!" His runesword in one hand and the scythe in the other he charged at another flapping beast, then moved towards Voilodion Ghagnasdiak who screeched and ran through a small doorway.

The tiger-creatures had bunched near the ceiling. Now they flew down again.

Corum made every effort to wrest one of the scythes from the beast who attacked him. Then his chance came when Elric took one in the back and sliced off his head. Corum picked up the dead thing's scythe and slashed at a third tiger-man who fell with his throat ripped out. Corum kicked the fallen scythe in Erekosë's direction.

The air was full of a sickening stench and black feathers stuck to the sweat and the blood on Corum's face and hands. He led the others back to the door through which they had entered the room and there they were able to defend themselves the better, for only so many of the creatures could come through at a time.

Corum felt mightily tired and he knew that he and his companions were bound to lose this struggle for, from his cover, Voilodion Ghagnasdiak was still throwing more globes into the room. Then he saw something fluttering behind the dwarf but, before he could make out what it was, a tiger-man blocked his view and he was forced to swing his body aside to avoid the blow of a scythe.

112

Then Corum heard a voice and when he next looked Voilo-dion Ghagnasdiak was struggling with something which clung to his face and Jhary-a-Conel stood there signalling to an astonished Elric who had just noticed him.

"Jhary!" shouted Corum.

"The one you came to save?" Elric slashed open the belly of yet another tiger-beast.

"Aye."

Elric was closest to Jhary and he prepared himself to cross the room. Jhary shouted back: "No No! Stay there!"

There was no need for the remark for Elric was once again engaged with two of the tiger-monsters who attacked him from both sides.

Jhary called out desperately. "You misunderstood what Bolorhiag told you."

Now Elric could see Jhary again, as could Erekosë. The black giant had, up to that time, been absorbed in the killing, seeming to take more pleasure in it than the others.

"Link arms! Corum in the centre!" Jhary called. "And you two draw your swords!"

Corum knew enough to guess that Jhary understood more than he had mentioned earlier. And now Elric was wounded in the leg.

"Hurry!" Jhary-a-Conel stood over the dwarf who strove to rip the thing from his face. "It is your only chance —— and mine!"

Elric seemed uncertain.

"He is wise, my friend," Corum told the albino. "He knows many things which we do not. Here, I will stand in the centre."

Erekosë seemed to awake from a trance. He looked at Corum over his bloody scythe, shook his great black head and then placed his right arm in Corum's, his sword in his left hand. Elric linked his left arm into Corum's right arm and drew his own strange sword.

And then Corum felt a power flow into his weary flesh and he almost laughed with delight at the sense of pleasure which filled him. Elric, himself, was laughing and even Erekosë smiled. They had combined. They had become the Three Who Are One and they moved as one, laughed as one, fought as one.

Although Corum did not fight, he felt as if he fought. He

113

felt that he had a sword in each hand and that he guided those hands.

The tiger-beasts fell back before the shrieking runeswords. They sought to escape this strange new power. They flapped wildly about the room.

Corum laughed in triumph. "Let us finish them!" And he knew they cried the same thing. No longer were their swords useless against the winged tiger-men. Instead they were invincible. Blood poured down as wounded beasts sought to escape, but none did escape.

As if weakened by the power released within it, the Vanishing Tower began to tremble. The floor tilted. Voilodion Ghagnasdiak's voice screamed from somewhere:

"The tower! The tower! This will destroy the tower!"

Corum could hardly keep his balance on the blood-slippery floor.

And then Jhary-a-Conel had entered the room, an expression of faint disgust on his face as he regarded the slaughter. "It is true. The sorcery we have worked today must have its effect. Whiskers —— to me!"

And then Corum realised that the creature which had clung to Voilodion Ghagnasdiak's face was the little black and white cat. Once again it had been the cause of their salvation. It flew to Jhary's shoulder and settled there, staring about with wide, green eyes.

Elric broke away from the other two and dashed into the other room to peer through the window slit. Corum heard him cry:

"We are in Limbo!"

Slowly Corum broke his own link with Erekosë. He did not have the energy to see what Elric meant, but he guessed that the Tower was in that timeless, spaceless place where once he had been in the Sky Ship. And it was swaying even more crazily now. He looked at the crumpled figure of the dwarf who had his hands to his face. Through the fingers welled fountains of blood.

Jhary went past Corum into the other room and spoke to Elric. As he returned Corum heard him say:

"Come, friend Elric, help me seek my hat."

"At such a time you look for a —— hat?"

"Aye." Jhary winked at Corum and stroked his cat. "Prince Corum —— Lord Erekosë —— will you come with me, too?"

114

They went past the weeping dwarf, down the narrow tunnel until they came to a flight of stairs. The stairs led towards a cellar. The tower quaked. With a lighted brand held aloft Jhary led them down the steps.

When a slab of masonry dislodged itself from the roof and fell at Elric's feet he said quietly: "I would prefer to seek a means of escape from the tower. If it falls now we shall be buried."

"Trust me, Prince Elric."

They came at length to a circular room with a huge metal door set in it.

"Voilodion's vault. Here you will find all the things you seek," said Jhary. "And I, I hope, will find my hat. The hat was specially made and is the only one which properly matches my other clothes ..."

"How do we open a door like that?" Erekosë sheathed his sword in an angry gesture. Then he drew it out again and put the point to the door. "It is made of steel, surely."

Jhary's voice was almost amused again. "If you linked arms again, my friends."

Corum offered Jhary an amused glance in spite of the danger.

"I will show you how the door may be opened," said Jhary.

And so they linked arms again and again the vast, exquisite sense of strength flowed through them and again they laughed to each other, feeling true fulfilment now that they were combined. Perhaps this was their destiny. Perhaps when they ceased to be individual heroes they would become the one thing again and they would experience happiness. It offered them hope, this thought.

Jhary said quietly, "And now, Prince Corum, if you would strike with your foot once upon the door ..."

Corum swung his foot and kicked at the steel and watched as the door fell down without resistance. He did not like to break the link with his fellow heroes. He could see how they could live as a single entity and know satisfaction. But he was forced to in order to enter the vault.

The tower shook and seemed to fall sideways and the four of them tumbled into Voilodion's vault to land amongst treasure.

Corum picked himself up. Elric was inspecting a golden

throne. Erekosë had picked up a battle-axe too big even for him to wield.

Here were the things Voilodion had stolen from all his victims as his tower had travelled through the planes.

Corum wondered if ever such a museum had ever existed before. He went from object to object inspecting them and marvelling. Meanwhile Jhary handed something to Elric and spoke with him. Corum heard Elric say to Jhary, "How can you know all this?"

Jhary made some vague reply and then bent with a cry of pleasure. He picked up his hat and began to slap at the dust which covered it. Then he saw another thing and picked that up. A goblet. "Take it," he told Corum. "It will prove useful, I think."

Jhary walked over to a corner and removed a small sack, placing it on his shoulder. There was a jewel chest near by and he delved through this until he discovered a ring. This he handed to Erekosë. "This is your reward, Erekosë, for in helping to free me from my captor." He spoke grandly but self-mockingly.

Even Erekosë smiled then. "I have the feeling you needed no help young man."

"You are mistaken, friend Erekosë. I doubt if I have ever been in greater peril." He took a lingering look around the room and then lost his footing as the floor tilted once more.

"We should take steps to leave," said Elric, the bundle of metal under his arm.

"Exactly." Jhary moved rapidly across the vault. "The last thing. In his pride Voilodion showed me his possessions, but he did not know the value of all of them."

Corum frowned. "What do you mean?"

"He killed the traveller who brought this with him. The traveller was right in assuming he had the means to stop the tower from vanishing, but he did not have time to use it before Voilodion had slain him." Jhary displayed the object. It was a small baton of a dull ochre colour. It hardly seemed valuable. "Here it is. The Runestaff. Hawkmoon had this with him when I travelled with him to the Dark Empire."

The Second Chapter

TO TANELORN

"What is the Runestaff?" Corum asked.

"I remember one description — but I am poor at naming and explaining things ..."

Elric almost smiled. "That has not escaped my attention."

Corum looked closely at the staff, unable to believe it had any special significance.

"It is an object," said Jhary, "which can only exist under a certain set of special and physical laws. In order to continue to exist, it must exert a field in which it can contain itself. That field must accord with those laws — the same laws under which we best survive."

Large slabs of masonry fell from the roof.

Erekosë growled. "The tower is breaking up."

Corum saw that Jhary was passing his hand in a stroking motion over the dull ochre staff, tracing out a pattern. "Please gather near me, my friends."

As the three closed in, the roof of the tower fell. Corum saw great blocks of stone descend to crush him and then he was staring at a blue sky breathing cool air and the ground was firm beneath his feet. Yet only a few inches on all sides of them there was blackness — the total blackness of Limbo. "Do not step outside this small area," Jhary said, "or you will be doomed." He frowned. "Let the Runestaff seek what we seek."

Corum knew his friend's voice and he knew that it was not as confident as usual.

The ground changed colour, the air was hot and then freezingly cold and Corum realised that they were moving rapidly through the planes as the Vanishing Tower had travelled, but they were not moving at random, he was sure of that.

Now there was sand beneath Corum's feet and a hot wind blowing in his face and Jhary was shouting: "Now!"

Running with the others into the blackness, Corum burst into sunlight and saw a glowing metallic sky.

"A desert," Erekosë said softly. "A vast desert ..."

On all sides rolled yellow dunes and the wind was sad as it whispered across them.

Jhary was plainly pleased with himself. "Do you recognise it, friend Elric?"

Elric was relieved. "Is it the Sighing Desert?"

"Listen."

Elric listened to the sad wind but he looked at something else. Corum turned his head and saw that Jhary had dropped the Runestaff, that it was fading.

"Are you all to come with me to the defence of Tanelorn?" Elric asked Jhary, doubtless expecting him to assent.

But Jhary shook his head. "No. We go the other way. We go to seek the device Theleb K'aarna activated with the help of the Lords of Chaos. Where lies it?"

Elric searched the dunes with his eyes. He frowned and then pointed hesitantly. "That way, I think."

"Then let us go to it now."

"But I must try to help Tanelorn!" Elric protested.

"You must destroy the device after we have used it, friend Elric, less Theleb K'aarna or his like try to activate it again."

"But Tanelorn..."

Corum listened with curiosity to the conversation. Why did Jhary know so much of Elric's world and its needs?

"I do not believe," said Jhary calmly, "that Theleb K'aarna and his beasts have yet reached the city."

"Not reached it! But so much time has passed!"

"Less than a day," said Jhary.

Corum wondered if that applied to them all or just to Elric's world. He sympathised with the albino as he rubbed his hand over his face and wondered whether to trust Jhary. Then he said: "Very well. I will take you to the machine."

"But if Tanelorn lies so near," Corum said to Jhary, "Why seek it elsewhere?"

"Because this is not the Tanelorn we wish to find," Jhary told him.

"It will suit me," Erekosë said almost humbly. "I will remain with Elric. Then, perhaps ..." There was longing in his eyes.

But Jhary was horrifid. "My friend," he said sadly, "already much of time and space is threatened with destruction. Eternal barriers could soon fall — the fabric of the multiverse could decay. You do not understand. Such a thing as has happened in the Vanishing Tower can only happen once in an eternity and even then it is dangerous to all concerned. You must do as I say. I promise that you will have just as good a chance of finding Tanelorn where I take you."

Erekosë bowed his head. "Very well."

"Come." Elric was impatient, already walking away from them. "For all your talk of Time, there is precious little left for me."

"For all of us," said Jhary feelingly.

They stumbled through the desert and the mourning wind found an echo of sadness in their own souls, but at last they came to a place of rocks, a natural amphitheatre which had in its centre a deserted camp. Tent flaps slapped as the wind blew them, but it was not the tent which drew their attention, it was the great bowl in the centre of the amphitheatre — a bowl which contained something far stranger than anything Corum had seen in Gwlâs-cor-Gwrys or in the world of Lady Jane Pentallyon. It had many planes and curves and angles of many colours and it dizzied him to look upon it too long.

"What is it?" he murmured.

"A machine," Jhary told him, "used by the ancients. It is what I have been seeking to take us to Tanelorn."

"But why not go with Elric to *his* Tanelorn?"

"We have the geography but we still need the time and the dimension," Jhary said. "Bear with me, Corum for, unless we are stopped, we should soon see the Tanelorn we seek."

"And we shall find aid against Glandyth?"

"That I cannot tell you."

Jhary went up to the machine in the bowl and he walked around it as if familiar with it. He seemed satisfied. He began to trace patterns on the bowl and these brought responses in the machine. Something deep within it began to pulse like a heart. The planes and curves and angles began to shift subtly and change colour. A sense of urgency came about Jhary's movements then. He made Corum and Erekosë stand with their backs pressed against the bowl and he took a small vial from his jerkin, handing it to Elric.

"When we have departed," said Jhary, "hurl this through the top of the bowl, take your horse which I still see yonder

119

and ride as fast as you can for Tanelorn. Follow these instructions perfectly and you will serve us all."

Gingerly, Elric took the vial. "Very well."

Jhary smiled a secret smile as he stood beside the other two. "And please give my compliments to my brother Moonglum."

Elric's crimson eyes widened. "You know him? What ...?"

"Farewell, Elric. We shall doubtless meet many times in the future, through we may not recognise each other."

Elric stood there, his white face stained by the light from the bowl.

"And that will be for the best, I suppose," Jhary added under his breath, looking at the albino with some sympathy.

But Elric was gone, as was the desert, as was the machine in the bowl.

Then something like an invisible hand threw them backwards.

Jhary sighed with satisfaction. "The machine is destroyed. That is good."

"But how may we return to our own plane?" Corum asked. They were surrounded by tall, waving grass — grass so high that it grew over their heads. "Where is Erekosë?"

"Gone on. Gone down his own road to Tanelorn," Jhary said. He looked at the sun. He took a bunch of the thick grass and wiped his face with it. There was dew on the grass and it refreshed him. "As we must now go down ours."

"Tanelorn is close?" Excitement suffused Corum. "Is it close, Jhary?"

"It is close. I feel its closeness."

"This is your city? You know its inhabitants?"

"This is my city. Tanelorn is ever my city. But this Tanelorn I do not know. I think I know of it, however — I hope I do or all my poor scheming will be for nothing."

"What are those schemes, Jhary? You must tell me more."

"I can tell you little. I knew of Elric's plight because I once rode with Elric — still do as far as he is concerned. Also I knew how to aid Erekosë, because I was once — or shall be — his friend, too. But it is not wisdom which guides me, Prince Corum. It is instinct. Come."

And he led the way through the tall, waving grass as if he followed as well-marked road.

The Third Chapter

THE CONJUNCTION OF THE MILLION SPHERES

And there was Tanelorn.

It was a blue city and it gave off a strong blue aura which merged with the expanse of the blue sky which framed it, but its buildings were of such a variety of shades of blue as to make them seem many-coloured. These tall spires and domes clustered together and intersected and adjoined each other and rose in wild spirals and curves, seeming to fling themselves joyfully at the heavens as if silently delighting in their own blue beauty, in all their colours from near-black to pale violet, in all their shapes of shining metal.

"It is not a mortal settlement," whispered Corum Jhaelen Irsei as he emerged with Jhary-a-Conel from the tall grass and drew his scarlet robe about him, feeling insignificant beneath the splendour of the city.

"I'll grant you that," said Jhary almost grimly. "It is not a Tanelorn which I have seen before. Why this is almost sinister, Corum ..."

"It is beautiful and it is wondrous, but it might almost be some false Tanelorn or some counter-Tanelorn, or some Tanelorn existing in an utterly different logic ..."

"I hardly follow you. You spoke of peace. Well, this Tanelorn is peaceful. You said that there were many Tanelorns and that they have existed before the beginning of time and will exist when time is ended. And if this Tanelorn is stranger than some you know, what of that?"

Jhary drew a heavy breath. "I believe I have some inkling of the truth now. If Tanelorn exists upon the only area in the multiverse not subject to flux, then it might have other purposes than to act as a resting place for weary heroes and the like ..."

"You think we are in danger there?"

"Danger? It depends what you regard as dangerous. Some wisdom may be dangerous to one man and not to another. Danger is contained in safety, as you have discovered, and

safety in danger. The nearest we ever come to knowing truth
is when we are witness to a paradox and therefore — I should
have considered this before — Tanelorn must be a paradox,
too. We had best enter the city, Corum, and learn why we
have been drawn here."

Corum hesitated. "Mabelode threatens to vanquish Law.
Glandyth-a-Krae aims to conquer my plane. Rhalina is lost.
We have much to sacrifice if we have made a mistake, Jhary."

"Aye. All."

"Then should we not first make certain that we are not
victims of some cosmic deceit."

Jhary turned and laughed aloud. "And how may we decide
that, Corum Jhaelen Irsei?"

Corum glared at Jhary and then lowered his eyes. "You are
right. We will enter this Tanelorn."

They crossed a lawn made blue by the light from the city
and they stood at the beginning of a wide avenue lined with
blue plants and breathed air which was not quite like the air
of any of the planes they had visited.

And Corum began to weep at the sight of so much marvellous beauty, falling to his knees as if in worship, feeling that
he would give his life to it willingly. And Jhary, standing beside his friend and placing a hand on his bowed shoulder,
murmured: "Ah, this is still truly Tanelorn."

Corum's very body seemed lighter as he and Jhary wandered down the avenue and looked for the inhabitants of
Tanelorn. Corum began to feel sure that there would be help
here, that Mabelode could, after all, be defeated, that his folk
and the folk of Lywm-an-Esh could be stopped from slaying
one another. And yet, though they wandered long, no citizens
of Tanelorn emerged to greet them. All there was was silence.

At the end of the avenue Corum now made out a shape
standing framed against a complicated fountain of blue water. The shape seemed to be that of a statue, the first represen-
tation of its kind Corum had seen in the city. And there was a
slight suggestion of familiarity about it which made him begin to hope for, in the back of his mind, he equated this statue
with salvation, though he did not know why.

He began to walk more swiftly until Jhary held him back, a
restraining hand on his arm. "Rush not, Corum, in Tanelorn."

The statue's detail became clearer as they advanced.

It was more barbaric in appearance than the rest of the city and it was predominantly green rather than blue. It did not seem to be of the same manufacture as the spires and the domes. It stood upon four legs arranged at each corner of its torso. It had four arms, two folded and two at its side. It had a large, human head but no nose. Instead, its nostrils were set directly into the head. The mouth was much wider than a human mouth and it was moulded so that it grinned. The eyes glittered and they too were completely unlike human eyes but rather resembled clusters of jewels.

"The eyes ..." Corum murmured, drawing still closer.

"Aye." Jhary knew what he meant.

The statue was not much taller than Corum and its whole body was encrusted with the dark, glowing jewels. He reached out to touch it but then stopped, for he had seen one of the folded arms and realisation was beginning to freeze his bones. On the right arm was a six-fingered hand. But on the left arm was no hand at all. The mate of the right hand was attached to Corum's wrist. He tried to retreat, his heart beating and his head pounding so that he could hear nothing else.

Slowly the grin on the statue's alien face widened still further. Slowly the hands at the sides came up towards Corum.

Then came the voice.

Never had Corum heard such a mixture of sound. Intelligent, savage, humorous, barbaric, cold, warm, soft and harsh, there were a thousand qualities in it as it said:

"The key may still not be mine until it is offered willingly."

The faceted eyes, twins of the one in Corum's skull, gleamed and shifted, while still the other two arms remained folded and the four legs remained as if paralysed.

In his shock, Corum could not speak. He was as petrified as the being seemed to be. Jhary stepped up beside him.

Quietly the dandy said: "You are Kwll."

"I am Kwll."

"And Tanelorn is your prison?"

"It has been my prison ..."

"... for only Timeless Tanelorn may hold a being of your power. I understand."

"But even Tanelorn cannot hold me unless I am incomplete."

Jhary lifted Corum's limp left arm. He touched the

six-fingered hand which was grafted there. "And this will make you complete."

"It is the key to my release. But the key may still not be mine until it is offered willingly."

"And you have worked for this, have you not, through the power of your brain which is not held by Tanelorn. It was not the Balance which allowed Elric and Erekosë to join this part of them called Corum. It was you, for only you or your brother are strong enough, though you be prisoners, to defy the essential laws — the Law of the Balance."

"Only Kwll and Rhynn are so strong, for only one law rules them."

"And you broke it. Eternities ago, you broke it. You fought each other and Rhynn struck off your hand while Kwll, you took out Rhynn's eye. You forgot your vows to each other — the sole vows you would ever consider obeying — and Rhynn, he —"

"He brought me here to Tanelorn and here I have remained, through all those cycles, those many cycles."

"And Rhynn, your brother? What punishment did you decree he suffer?"

"That he search, without rest, for his missing eye, but that he must find the eye alone, not with the hand."

"And the eye and hand have always been together."

"As they are now."

"And so Rhynn has never succeeded."

"It is as you say, mortal. You know much."

"It is because," answered Jhary, seeming to speak to himself, "because I am one of those mortals doomed to immortality."

"The key must be offered willingly," said Kwll again.

"Was it your shadow I saw in the Flamelands?" Corum asked suddenly, moving back from the being on trembling legs. "Was it you I saw on the hill from Castle Erorn?"

"You saw my shadow, aye. But you did not, could not see me. And I saved your life in the Flamelands and elsewhere. I used my hand and I killed your enemies."

"They were not enemies." Corum clutched the six-fingered hand to him, looking at it with loathing. "And you gave the hand the power to summon the dead to my aid?"

"The hand has that power. It is nothing. A trick."

"And you did this merely with your brain — your thoughts?"

"I have done more than that. The key must be offered willingly. I cannot force you, mortal, to give me back my hand."

"And if I keep it?"

"Then I shall have to wait through the Cycle of Cycles once again until the Million Spheres are again in conjunction. Have you not understood that?"

"I have come to understand it," Jhary said gravely. "How else could so many planes open to mortals? How else could so many discover fragments of wisdom usually denied them? How else could three aspects of the same entity exist upon the same plane? How else could I remember other existences? It is the Conjunction of the Million Spheres. A conjunction which takes place so rarely that a being could think he lived for eternity and still not witness it. And when that conjunction takes place, I have heard, old laws are broken and new ones established — the very nature of space and time and reality are altered."

"Would that mean the end of Tanelorn?" Corum asked.

"Perhaps even the end of Tanelorn," said Kwll, "But of that alone I am not sure. The key must be offered willingly."

"And what do I release if I offer the key?" Corum said to Jhary.

Jhary-a-Conel shook his head and took his little black and white cat partly from within his jerkin and stroked its head, deep in thought.

"You release Kwll," said Kwll. "You release Rhynn. Each has paid his price."

"What shall I do, Jhary?"

"I do not ..."

"Shall I strike a bargain? Shall I say that he may have his hand if he will help us against the King of the Swords, help us restore peace to my land, help us find Rhalina?"

Jhary shrugged.

"What shall I do, Jhary?"

But Jhary refused to reply, so Corum looked directly into the face of Kwll. "I will give you back your hand on condition that you will use your great powers to destroy the rule of Chaos on the Fifteen Planes, that you will slay Mabelode, the King of the Swords, that you will help me discover where my love, the lady Rhalina, lies, that you will help me bring peace to my own world so that it may dwell under the rule of Law. Say you will do this."

"I will do it."

"Then willingly I offer you the key. Take your hand, Lost God, for it has brought me little but pain!"

"You fool!" It was Jhary shouting. "I told you that ..."

But his voice was faint and growing yet fainter. Corum relived the torment he had suffered in the forest, when Glandyth had struck off his hand. He screamed as the pain came to his wrist once more and then there was fire in his face and he knew that Kwll had plucked his brother's jewelled eye from his skull, now that his powers were restored. Red darkness swam in his brain. Red fire drained his energy. Red pain consumed his flesh.

"... they obey only one law — the law of loyalty to each other!" Jhary shouted. "I prayed your decision would not be this."

"I am ..." Corum spoke thickly, looking at the stump where the hand had been, touching the smooth flesh where his eye had been. "I am a cripple once again."

"And I am whole." Kwll's strange voice had not changed in tone, but his jewelled body glowed the brighter and he stretched his four legs and all his four arms and he sighed with pleasure. "Whole."

In one of his hands the Lost God held his brother's eye and he held it so that it shone in the blue light from the city. "And free," he said. "Soon, brother, we shall range again the Million Spheres as we always ranged before our fight — in joy and in delight at all the variety of things. We two are the only beings who really know pleasure! I must find you, brother! "

"The bargain," said Corum insistently, ignoring Jhary. "You told me you would help me, Kwll."

"Mortal, I make no bargains, I obey no laws save the one of which you have already learned. I care not for Law nor for Chaos nor for the Cosmic Balance. Kwll and Rhynn exist for the love of existence and nothing else and we do not concern ourselves with the illusory struggles of petty mortals and their pettier gods. Do you not know that you *dream* of these gods — that you are stronger than they — that when you are fearful, why then you bring fearsome gods upon yourselves? Is this not evident to you?"

"I do not understand your words. I say that you must keep your bargain."

"I go now to seek my brother Rhynn and toss this eye somewhere where he may easily find it and so be free like me."

"Kwll! You owe me much!"

"Owe? I acknowledge no debts save my debt to myself to follow my own desires and those of my brother. Owe? What do I owe?"

"Without me, you would not now be free."

"Without my previous aid you would not now be alive. Be grateful!"

"I have been ill-used by gods, Kwll. I weary of it. A pawn of Chaos and then Law and now Kwll. At least Law acknowledges that power must have responsibility. You are no better than the Lords of Chaos!"

"Untrue! We harm no one, Rhynn and I. What pleasure is there in playing these silly games of Law and Chaos, of manipulating the fate of mortals and demigods? You mortals are used because you wish to be used, because *you* can then place the responsibility of your actions upon these gods of yours. Forget all gods — forget me. You'll be happier."

"Yet you did use me, Kwll. That you must admit."

Kwll turned his back on Corum, tossing a dark, many-barbed spear into the air and making it vanish. "I use many things — I use my weapons — but I do not feel indebted to them once they are no longer of use."

"You are unjust, Kwll!"

"Justice?" Kwll shook with laughter. "What is that?"

Corum poised himself to spring at the Lost God, but Jhary held him back. The dandy said: "If you train a dog to fetch your quarry for you, Kwll, you reward it, do you not? Then, if you need it, it will fetch for you again."

Kwll spun round on his four legs, his faceted eyes glittering. "But if it will not, then one trains a new dog."

"I am immortal," Jhary said. "And I will make it my business to warn all the other dogs that there is naught to be gained from running the Lost Gods' errands ..."

"I have no further need of dogs."

"Have you not? Even you cannot anticipate what will come about after the Conjunction of the Million Spheres."

"I could destroy you, mortal who is immortal."

"You would be as petty as those you despise."

"Then I will help you." Kwll flung back his jewelled head and laughed so that even Tanelorn seemed to shake with his mirth. "It will save me time, I think."

"You will keep your bargain?" Corum demanded.

"I admit no bargain. But I will help you." Kwll leapt forward suddenly and seized Corum under one arm and Jhary under another. "First, to the Realm of the King of the Swords."

And blue Tanelorn was gone and all around them rose the unstable stuff of Chaos, dancing like lava in an erupting volcano, and through it Corum saw Rhalina.

But Rhalina was five thousand feet high.

The Fourth Chapter

THE KING OF THE SWORDS

Kwll set them down and stared at the gigantic woman. "It is not flesh," he said. "It is a castle."

It was a castle fashioned to resemble Rhalina. But what had built it and for what purpose? And where was Rhalina herself?

"We'll visit the castle," Kwll said, stepping through the leaping Chaos matter as another might pass through smoke. "Stay closely with me."

They walked on until they came to a flight of white stone steps which led up and up into the distance and ended finally at a doorway set in the navel of the towering statue. His four legs moving surprisingly clumsily, Kwll began to climb the steps. He was singing to himself.

At last they reached the top and entered the circular doorway to find themselves in a great hall illuminated by light which poured downward from the distant head.

And in the centre of the light stood a great group of creatures, all armed as if ready for battle. These creatures were both malformed and beautiful and they wore a variety of kinds of armour and bore a variety of weapons. Some had heads which resembled those of beasts, while some looked like beautiful women. They were all smiling at the three who entered the chamber. And Corum knew them for the gathered Dukes of Hell — those who served Mabelode, the King of the Swords.

Kwll, Corum and Jhary paused at the doorway. Kwll bowed and smiled back and they seemed a little astonished to see him but plainly did not recognise what he was. Their ranks parted and there stood two more figures.

One of them was tall and naked but for a light robe. His white skin was smooth and without hair and his body was perfectly proportioned. Long, fair hair flowed to his shoulders, but he had no face. Completely featureless skin covered the head where the eyes and the nose and the mouth would have been.

Corum knew this must be Mabelode, who was called the Faceless.

The other figure was Rhalina.

"I hoped you would come," said the King of the Swords, though he had no lips to form the words. "That is why I built my castle — to act as a lure to you when you returned to seek your lady. Mortals are so loyal!"

"Aye, we are that," agreed Corum. "Are you safe, Rhalina?"

"I am safe — and my fury keeps me sane," she said. "I thought you dead, Corum, when the Sky Ship was wrecked. But this creature told me it was unlikely. Have you found help? It seems not. You have lost your hand and your eye again, I see." She spoke flatly.

Tears came into Corum's eye. "Mabelode will pay for having discomforted you," he told her.

The faceless god laughed and his dukes laughed with him. It was as if beasts had learned the power of laughter. Mabelode reached behind Rhalina and drew out a great golden sword which dazzled them with its light. "I swore that I would avenge both Arioch and Xiombarg," said Mabelode the Faceless. "I swore I would not risk my life or my position until you, Corum, were in my power. And when Duke Teer was tricked by you" (Duke Teer lowered his porcine head at this) "into fighting our servant Glandyth, whom I also allowed to play a part in preparing my trap, then you almost fled into my snare. But something happened. Only the girl was caught and you and the other thing vanished. So I used the girl, this time, as bait. And I waited. And you came. And now I may administer your punishment. My first intention is to mould your flesh a little, mixing it with that of your companions until you become more foul to look upon than anything of mine you affect to loathe. As this I will let you linger a year or two — or however long your little brain can endure it — and then I will restore you to your original forms and make

129

you hate each other and lust for each other at the same time —
You are already experienced, I think, in something I can do in
that direction. Then ..."

"What mundane imaginations these Lords of Chaos have,"
said Kwll in his many-toned voice. "What modest ambitions
they entertain! What petty dreams they dream." He laughed.
"They are hardly men, let alone gods."

The Dukes of Hell fell silent and turned their heads to
watch their king.

Mabelode held his golden sword in his two hands and from
it burst a thousand shadows, all twisting and dancing in the
air, all suggesting shapes to Corum, but shapes which he
could not name.

"My power is not mundane, creature! What are you that
you can mock the most powerful of the Sword Rulers, Mabelode the Faceless?"

"I do not mock," said Kwll. "I am Kwll." He reached into
the air and took a several-bladed sword from it. "I state that
which is evident."

"Kwll is dead," said Mabelode, "As Rhynn is dead. Dead.
You are a charlatan. Your conjuring is not entertaining."

"I am Kwll."

"Kwll is dead."

"I am Kwll."

Three of the Dukes of Hell rushed at the being then, their
swords raised.

"Slay him," said Mabelode, "so that I may begin to have
the pleasure of my vengeance."

Kwll plucked two more many-bladed swords from the air.
He let the swords of the Dukes of Hell fall upon his jewelled
body before casually skewering each one of them and tossing
them away so that they vanished.

"Kwll ..." he said. "The power of the multiverse is mine."

"No single being can have such power!" Mabelode shouted.
"The Cosmic Balance denies it."

"I do not obey the Cosmic Balance, however," said Kwll
reasonably. He turned to Corum and Jhary and he handed
Corum the Eye of Rhynn. "I will dispense with these. Take
my brother's eye to your own plane and cast it into the sea.
There'll be no need for you to do else."

"And Glandyth?"

"Surely you can deal with a fellow mortal without my aid.
You grow lazy, mortal."

130

"But — Rhalina ..."

"Ah."

Kwll's hand seemed to extend through the gathered ranks of the Dukes of Hell, past King Mabelode the Faceless, and pluck Rhalina from the Sword Ruler's side.

"There."

Rhalina sobbed in Corum's arms.

Corum heard Mabelode cry: "Summon all my strength! Summon all the creatures of all the planes who are pledged to me. Ready yourselves, my Dukes of Hell! Chaos must be defended!"

Jhary shouted back at him: "Do you fear one being, King of the Swords? Just one?"

Mabelode's golden sword flickered in his hand. His back seemed bowed, his voice was low. "I fear Kwll," he said.

"You are wise to do so," said Kwll. He waved one of his hands. "Now, let us dismiss all these silly trappings and concern ourselves with the fight."

The castle shaped like Rhalina began to melt around them. The Dukes of Hell cried out in terror, their shapes changing as they sought to find the one which would serve them best. Mabelode the Faceless began to increase in size until his huge, faceless head loomed over them..

Fierce colours slashed the skies. Pools of darkness appeared. Screams were heard and grunts and sucking sounds. From all points came things which hopped and things which slithered and things which galloped and things which flew and things which walked — all things of Chaos come to aid King Mabelode.

Kwll tapped Jhary on the shoulder and the dandy disappeared.

Corum gasped. "Even you cannot go against the entire strength of Chaos! I regret my bargain. I release you from it!"

"I made no bargain." Two hands came out and tapped Corum and Rhalina. Corum felt himself being drawn away from the Realm of Chaos.

"They will destroy you, Kwll!"

"I admit I have not fought for some time, but doubtless I will remember my old skills."

Corum glimpsed the roaring terror that was Chaos hurling itself upon the Lost God. "No ... "

He struggled to draw his own sword, but he was falling

131

now. Falling as he had fallen once before when the Sky Ship had been wrecked. But this time he held tightly to Rhalina.

Even as his senses clouded he kept his grip upon her arm until he heard her calling his name.

"Corum! Corum! You pain me!"

His eyes were closed. He opened them. She and he were standing on blackened stone and the sea was all around them. He did not recognise the place at first, for the castle was no longer there. And then he remembered that Glandyth had burned it.

They stood on Moidel's Mount.

The tide was beginning to go out and they glimpsed the causeway as it was slowly uncovered.

"Look," said Rhalina, pointing towards the forest.

He looked and he saw several corpses.

"So the strife continues," he said. He was about to help her to climb down when he looked at the thing he had clutched even as he had clutched Rhalina with his single hand. It was the Eye of Rhynn.

He drew back his arm and flung it far out into the sea. It flashed in the air and then disappeared beneath the waves.

"I am not sorry to see that dismissed at last," he said.

The Fifth Chapter

THE LAST OF GLANDYTH

When they had crossed the causeway and reached the mainland they could better distinguish the corpses sprawled near the edge of the forest. They were of their old enemies, the Pony Tribesmen. They had fought each other savagely and for some time, by all the signs. They lay in their furs and their necklets and bracelets of copper and bronze with their crude swords and axes in their hands, each man bearing at least a dozen wounds. They had plainly been gripped by the

Cloud of Contention which the Nhadragh's sorcery had brought to the land. Corum bent down and inspected the nearest corpse.

"Not dead long," he said. "It means the sickness is still strong. And yet it does not touch us. Perhaps it takes time to enter our brains. Ah, the poor folk of Lywm-an-Esh — my poor Vadhagh ..."

A movement in the trees.

Corum drew his sword, feeling for the first time the lack of his left hand and right eye. He felt off-balance. Then he grinned in relief.

It was Jhary-a-Conel leading three of the dead tribesmen's ponies by their bridle ropes.

"Not the most comfortable beasts to ride, but better than walking. Where do you head for, Corum. For Halwyg?"

Corum shook his head. "I have been thinking of the only positive deed we can try to perform. There's little to be done in Halwyg. I doubt if Glandyth has yet set up his court there for, doubtless, he still hunts for us on other planes. We'll go to Erorn, I think. There is a boat there we can use and it will take us to the Nhadragh Isles."

"Where the sorcerer dwells who has put this spell upon the world."

"Just so."

Jhary-a-Conel stroked his cat under its chin. "Your idea is sound, Corum Jhaelen Irsei. Let us make speed."

Soon they were mounted on the shaggy ponies and were driving them as hard as they could do through the woods of Bro-an-Vadhagh. Twice they were forced to hide while small groups of Vadhagh hunted each other. Once they witnessed a massacre, but there was nothing they could do to save the victims.

Corum was relieved to sight the towers of Castle Erorn at long last, for he had wondered if Glandyth or some other had destroyed it again. The castle was as they had left it. The snow had all melted and a mild spring was beginning to touch the trees and shrubs. Gratefully they entered the castle.

But they had forgotten the retainers.

The retainers had not resisted the sickness long. They found two corpses just inside the doorway, horribly butchered. Others were elsewhere in the castle and all had been murdered save one — the last survivor, his aggression had turned to self-hatred and he had hanged himself in one of the rooms of music. His presence caused the fountains and the crystals to make a sour, dreadful sound which almost drove Corum, Rhalina and Jhary back out of the castle.

The work of disposing of the corpses done, Corum took the passage down to the large sea-cave below the castle. Here was the little boat in which he and Rhalina had sailed for pleasure in the short-lived days of peace. It was ready for immediate use.

Rhalina and Jhary brought down the provisions while Corum checked the rigging and the sail. They waited for the tide to turn and then sailed beneath the great, rugged arch of the sea-cave and out into open water. It would be two days before they sighted the first of the Nhadragh Isles.

With only the sea surrounding him, Corum thought about his adventures upon the different planes. He had entered so many worlds he had lost count of them. Were there really a Million Spheres, each sphere containing a number of planes? It was hard to conceive it so many worlds. And on each world a struggle was taking place.

"Are there no worlds which know permanent peace?" he asked Jhary as he took over the rudder of the boat while the dandy adjusted the sail. "Are there none, Jhary?"

The dandy shrugged. "Perhaps there are, though I have never seen one. Perhaps it is not my fate to see one. But it is basic to Nature to know struggle of some kind, surely?"

"Some creatures live in peace all their lives."

"Aye, some do. There is a legend that once there was only one world — one planet like ours — which was tranquil and perfect. But something evil invaded it and it learnt strife and in learning strife it created other examples of itself where strife could flourish the better. But there are many legends which say the past was perfect or that the future will be perfect. I have seen many pasts and many futures. None of them were perfect, my friend."

Corum felt the boat rock and he tightened his grip on the rudder. The waves became larger and the sea was choppy.

Rhalina pointed into the distance. "The Wading God — see! He goes towards our coast, still fishing."

"Perhaps the Wading God knows peace," said Corum when the sea settled and the giant had gone.

Jhary stroked the head of his cat. The little creature looked nervously at the water. "I think not," said Jhary quietly.

134

Another day went by before they saw the outer islands of the group. They were predominantly dark green and brown and as they sailed by them they saw the black ruins of the towns and the castles which the Mabden had fired when they had come a-reaving to the Nhadragh Isles. Once or twice a shambling figure would wave to them from a beach but they ignored him, for doubtless the Cloud of Contention had touched those who were left of the Nhadragh.

"There," said Corum. "That large island. It is Maliful where lies the city of Os and the Nhadragh sorcerer Ertil. I think I feel the Cloud of Contention begin to gnaw again at my brain ..."

"Then we had best hurry and do our work, if we can," Jhary said.

They landed the small boat on a stony, deserted beach quite close to Os whose walls they could already see.

"Go Whiskers," murmured Jhary to his cat, "show us the way to the sorcerer's keep."

The cat spread its wings and flew high into the air, hovering to keep pace with them as they moved cautiously towards the city. Then, as they climbed over the rubble of what had once been a gateway and began to make their way through piles of weed-grown masonry, the cat flew to the squat building with the yellow dome upon its roof. It flew twice around the dome and then came back to settle on Jhary's shoulder.

Corum felt a twinge of annoyance at the cat. It was reasonless anger and he knew what caused it. He began to run towards the squat building.

There was only one entrance and it was filled with a hard, wooden door.

"To break that," whispered Jhary, "would be to make our presence known . Look, here — steps lead up the side."

A flight of stone steps led to the roof and up these the three went, Rhalina following in the wake of the men.

Together they crept up to the dome and peered inside. At first it was hard to make out what was in there. They saw the clutter of parchments and animal cages and cauldrons. But there was a form moving about in one corner. It could only be the sorcerer.

"I'm tired of this caution!" Corum shouted. "Let's end it now!" With a yell he reversed his sword hilt and struck

135

heavily at the dome. It groaned and a crack appeared. He struck again and the stuff shattered, falling into the room.

But Corum had released a stink which drove them back for a few yards until it had dispersed in the cleaner outer air. Corum, feeling the unreasoning fury rising in him again, dashed to the edge of the broken dome and leapt through the hole he had made, landing with a crash upon the scored table below.

Sword ready, he glared around him.

And what he saw drove the fury from his head. It was the Nhadragh, Ertil.

The corrupt sorcerer had plainly succumbed to his own spell. There was foam on his lips. His dark eyes rolled.

"I killed them," he said, "as I will kill you. They would not obey me — so I killed them."

With his one remaining arm he held up his severed leg. Another leg and an arm bled near by.

"I killed them!"

Corum turned away, kicking out at the bubbling cauldron, the vials of herbs and chemicals, scattering them about the room.

"I killed them!" babbled the sorcerer. His voice rose to a shriek and then subsided. The blood was pouring from his body. He would only live a few seconds more.

"How made you the Cloud of Contention?" Corum asked him.

Weakly Ertil grinned and gestured with the severed leg. "There — the censer. Only a little censer — but it has destroyed you all."

"Not all." Corum grabbed the censer by its chains and immersed it in one of the cauldrons. Green steam boiled from its sides and evil faces flickered in that steam for a moment before fading away.

"I have destroyed that which destroyed so many of my folk, sorcerer," Corum said.

Ertil looked up at him through glazed eyes. "Then destroy me, too, Vadhagh. I deserve it."

Corum shook his head. "I'll let you continue to die in the manner you chose."

From above came Jhary's voice.

"Corum!"

The Prince in the Scarlet Robe looked up and saw Jhary's face framed in the hole in the dome. Jhary looked daunted.

136

"What is it, Jhary?"

"Glandyth must have sensed the decline in the sorcerer's sanity."

"What mean you?"

"He comes, Corum. His beasts still bear him."

Corum sheathed his sword and jumped from the table. "I'll join you below. I can't get back that way."

He stepped over what was left of Ertil the Nhadragh and he pulled open the door. As he went down the stairs he heard the voices of the caged animals chattering and crying, begging him to release them.

Outside Jhary was already waiting for him with Rhalina. Corum took Rhalina and made her enter the building.

"Stay there, Rhalina. It is a foul place but it offers greater safety. Please stay there."

Black wings beat in the sky. Glandyth was near.

Corum and Jhary ran out until they stood in what had once been a square. Now piles of rubble filled it.

The Denledhyssi were fewer in number. Doubtless some had died in the encounter with Duke Teer. But there were still a dozen black monsters in the air above Os.

A blood-curdling yell of triumph suddenly sounded from the sky and it echoed through the ruined city.

"Corum!"

It was Glandyth-a-Krae and he had seen his enemy.

"Where are your sorcerous hand and eye, Shefanhow? Gone back to the netherworld you conjured them from, eh?"

Glandyth began to laugh.

"So, after all, we are to die at the hands of the Mabden," Corum said quietly as he watched the black beasts land on the far side of the square. "Prepare to perish, Jhary."

They waited with their swords ready as Glandyth dismounted from his Chaos monster and began to tramp across the ruins, his Denledhyssi at his back.

Thinking that he might save Jhary and Rhalina, Corum called to the huge man: "Will you fight me fairly, Earl Glandyth? Will you tell your men to stand back while we battle?"

Glandyth-a-Krae adjusted his bulky furs on his back and he tilted his helm further over his red face. Laughter exploded from his thick lips. "If you think it is fair for me to fight a wretch with but one hand and one eye, yes, I'll fight you, Corum." He winked at his men. "Stand back as he says. I'll let you have his other hand and his other eye in a little while."

The barbarians yelled with mirth at their leader's jest.

The Mabden earl came closer until only a few yards separated them. He glowered at the Vadhagh. "You have caused me much discomfort of late, Shefanhow. But now my pleasure makes me forget it all. I am most glad to see you." He drew his great war-axe from his belt and slid his sword from its scabbard. "We shall complete what was begun in the woods at Castle Erorn."

He took a step forward but then a frightened yell from his men made him stop and glance back.

The black beasts were rising into the air and flying eastwards. And as they flew they vanished.

"Going back to Chaos," Corum told Glandyth. "Their master needs them, for he is hard-pressed. If I kill you, Glandyth, will your men let me free?"

Glandyth grinned his wolf grin. "They love me greatly do my Denledhyssi."

"So I have little to gain," Corum said. "One moment." He murmured to Jhary: "Take Rhalina now. Get to the boat. Even if I am killed the Denledhyssi have no transportation now and will not be able to follow you. It is the wisest thing, Jhary, do not deny that."

Jhary sighed. "I do not deny it. I will do as you say. I go."

"You will let him leave Os, will you not?" Corum said.

Glandyth shrugged. "Very well. If we become bored we can always hunt him down later. And do not think that I mind the loss of a few Chaos beasts. I have my own sorcerer to conjure up something new if I need it."

"Ertil?"

Glandyth's unhealthy eyes narrowed. "What of Ertil?"

"He has killed himself. The Cloud of Contention reached even him."

"No matter. I will — haaiii!" The Earl of Krae flung himself suddenly at Corum, the battle-axe and the sword slashing from two sides.

Corum jumped back, caught his foot, fell as the axe whistled over his head. He rolled as the sword clashed down on the block of masonry where he had lain. He supported himself on the stump of his left hand and got to his feet, blocking a wild blow from the axe.

The barbarian was as strong and as swift as ever, for all his girth. His presence alone made Corum feel as weak as a child in comparison. He strove to take the offensive, but Glandyth allowed him no respite, forcing him further and further back over the rubble. Corum's only hope was that Jhary had managed to get Rhalina to the boat and that, by the time Glandyth slew him, they would be sailing back for Castle Erorn.

Both axe and sword came down on Corum's upraised blade and his arm went numb beneath the force of the blow. He slid his sword down the haft of the axe, trying to cut Glandyth's fingers, but the Earl of Krae withdrew the axe and aimed it at Corum's head.

Corum dodged and the axe sheared off the links of the byrnie on his left shoulder but only grazed the flesh.

Glandyth grinned. His foul breath was in Corum's face, his mad eyes were full of death-lust. He stabbed with his sword and Corum felt the steel slide into his thigh. He backed off and saw that there was blood running down the silver mail.

Panting, Glandyth paused, readying himself for the kill.

And Corum dashed in, struck with his blade at Glandyth's face and gashed his cheek before the barbarian's sword came up and pushed away his weapon.

Blood continued to pour from the wound in his thigh. Corum hobbled backward over the ruins, trying to put a little distance between himself and his enemy. Glandyth did not follow but stood there, relishing Corum's pain.

"I think I can still have the pleasure of making your death a slow one. Would you care to run a little way, Prince Corum, to purchase a few extra seconds of life?"

Corum straightened his back. He was almost fainting. He could say nothing. He stared at Glandyth through his single eye and then he took a step forward.

Glandyth chuckled. "I slew all your race, save you. Now, after much patient waiting, I can slay the last of your filthy kind."

Corum took another step forward.

Glandyth readied his weapons. "You want to die, eh?"

Corum swayed. He could hardly see the Earl of Krae. He raised his sword with difficulty and tried to take a further step.

"Come," said Glandyth, "come."

A shadow passed over the ruins. At first Corum thought he imagined it. He shook his head to try to clear it.

Glandyth had seen the shadow, too. His red mouth fell open in astonishment, his bloodshot eyes widened.

And while he stared up at the thing which cast the shadow, Corum fell forward behind his sword and plunged the steel into Glandyth's throat.

Glandyth made a hollow, gurgling sound and blood welled from his mouth.

"For my family," said Corum.

The shadow moved on. It was a giant who cast it. A giant with a great net which he cast down over the terrified men of the Denledhyssi and dragged them upward and hurled their bodies far out over the city. It was a giant with two glittering, jewelled eyes.

Corum fell down beside the corpse of Glandyth-a-Krae, looking up at the giant. "The Wading God," he said.

Jhary appeared beside him, staunching the blood from his thigh. "The Wading God," he said to Corum. "But he no longer fishes the seas of the world for he found what he sought."

"His soul?"

"His eye. The Wading God is Rhynn."

Corum's vision was even more blurred. But through a pink mist he saw Kwll come, a grin upon his jewelled head.

"Your Chaos gods are gone," said Kwll. "With my brother's help I slew them all and all their minions."

"I thank you," Corum said thickly. "And Lord Arkyn will thank you, too."

Kwll chuckled. "I think not."

"Why — why so?"

"For good measure we slew the Lords of Law as well. Now you mortals are free of gods on these planes."

"But Arkyn — Arkyn was good ..."

"Find the same good in yourselves if that is what you respect. It is the time of the Conjunciton of the Million Spheres and that means change — profound alterations in the nature of existence. Perhaps that was our function — to rid the Fifteen Planes of its silly gods and their silly schemes."

"But the Balance ...?"

"Let it swing up and down with a will. It has nothing to weigh now. You are on your own, mortal — you and your kind. Farewell."

Corum tried to speak again, but the pain in his thigh swamped all thought. At last he fainted.

Once more Kwll's many-toned voice sounded in his skull before his senses were engulfed completely.

"Now you can make your own destiny."

EPILOGUE

Again the land had healed and again mortals went about their business, repairing what had been destroyed. A new king was found for Lywm-an-Esh and the Vadhagh who had escaped death returned to their castles.

At Castle Erorn by the sea Corum Jhaelen Irsei, the Prince in the Scarlet Robe, recovered his health thanks to the potions of Jhary-a-Conel and the nursing of the Lady Rhalina and he found a new hobby for himself, remembering what he had seen at the doctor's house when trapped upon the plane of Lady Jane Pentallyon, which was the manufacture of artificial hands. He had yet to make one that satisfied him.

One day came Jhary-a-Conel in his hat with his bag on his back and his cat on his shoulder and he said good-bye to them with some reluctance. They begged him to stay, to enjoy the peace they had earned.

"For a world without gods is a world without much to fear," said Corum.

"That is true," Jhary agreed.

"Then stay," said the Lady Rhalina.

"But," said Jhary, "I go to seek worlds where gods still rule, for I am not suited to any other. And," he added, "I would hate it if I came to blame myself for my misfortunes. That would not do at all! Gods — a sense of an omniscience not far away — demons — destinies which cannot be denied — absolute evil — absolute good — I need it all."

Corum smiled. "Then go if you will and remember that we love you. But do not despair entirely of this world, Jhary. New gods can always be created."

This ends the Third and final

Book of Corum

Science Fantasy

The Mercurial Mind of
Michael Moorcock

Escape from present-day insanity to new, different, timeless worlds with Britain's most imaginative, most original
talent. The following titles are all available in Mayflower:

The History of the Runestaff:
Vol I   THE JEWEL IN THE SKULL   25p
Vol II   THE MAD GOD'S AMULET   17½p
Vol III   THE SWORD OF THE DAWN   20p
Vol IV   THE RUNESTAFF   25p

THE BLACK CORRIDOR   25p
THE STEALER OF SOULS   25p
STORMBRINGER   25p
THE SINGING CITADEL   25p
BEHOLD THE MAN   25p
THE FINAL PROGRAMME   25p
THE ETERNAL CHAMPION   25p
PHOENIX IN OBSIDIAN   25p
THE KNIGHT OF THE SWORDS   25p
THE TIME DWELLER   25p
THE QUEEN OF THE SWORDS   25p

MAYFLOWER SCIENCE FICTION BESTSELLERS

"Then the Earth grew old, its landscapes mellowing and showing signs of age, its ways becoming whimsical and strange in the manner of a man in his last years"

Michael Moorcock

☐ VIRGIN PLANET	Poul Anderson	25p
☐ VOICES FROM THE SKY	Arthur C. Clarke	25p
☐ WARLOCKS AND WARRIORS	Ed. by Douglas Hill	25p
☐ WORLDS OF THE IMPERIUM	Keith Laumer	20p
☐ THE MONITORS	Keith Laumer	25p
☐ GALACTIC ODYSSEY	Keith Laumer	20p
☐ A SPECTRE IS HAUNTING TEXAS	Fritz Leiber	30p
☐ THE SWORDS OF LANKHMAR	Fritz Leiber	30p
☐ DIMENSION OF MIRACLES	Robert Sheckley	25p
☐ THE TENTH VICTIM	Robert Sheckley	20p
☐ THE REPRODUCTIVE SYSTEM	John Sladek	25p

All these books are available at your local bookshop or newsagent: or can be ordered direct from the publisher. Just tick the titles you want and fill in the form below.

Write to Mayflower Cash Sales, P.O. Box 11, Falmouth, Cornwall. Please send cheque or postal order value of the cover price plus 6p for postage and packing.

Name ....

Address ....

....